SPECIAL MESSAGE TO READERS

This book is published by
THE ULVERSCROFT FOUNDATION,
a registered charity in the U.K., No. 264873

The Foundation was established in 1974 to provide funds to help towards research, diagnosis and treatment of eye diseases. Below are a few examples of contributions made by THE ULVERSCROFT FOUNDATION:

- ★ A new Children's Assessment Unit at Moorfield's Hospital, London.
- ★ Twin operating theatres at the Western Ophthalmic Hospital, London.
- ★ The Frederick Thorpe Ulverscroft Chair of Ophthalmology at the University of Leicester.
- ★ Eye Laser equipment to various eye hospitals.

If you would like to help further the work of the Foundation by making a donation or leaving a legacy, every contribution, no matter how small, is received with gratitude. Please write for details to:

THE ULVERSCROFT FOUNDATION,
The Green, Bradgate Road, Anstey,
Leicestershire, LE7 7FU. England.
Telephone: (0533) 364325

A CALL TO DIE

Ross MacAllister witnesses a fatal road accident. He is certain that the victim was deliberately run down, but his arguments do not convince the police. Then he learns that a second victim was killed in the same way at the same time—less than thirty miles away! He persuades his good friend Detective Inspector Gwyn Thomas that something is desperately wrong. And as the police swing into action, a faded actress is found battered to death. Then Detective Inspector Thomas suddenly realises that Ross MacAllister is missing!

*Books by Christopher Coram
in the Linford Mystery Library:*

**A CALL TO MURDER
A CALL TO DIE**

CHRISTOPHER CORAM

A CALL TO DIE

Complete and Unabridged

LINFORD
Leicester

First Linford Edition
published February 1990

Copyright © 1969 by Christopher Coram
All rights reserved

British Library CIP Data

Coram, Christopher, *1936*–
A call to die.—Large print ed.—
Linford mystery library
I. Title
823'.914[F]

ISBN 0-7089-6842-2

Published by
F. A. Thorpe (Publishing) Ltd.
Anstey, Leicestershire

Set by Rowland Phototypesetting Ltd.
Bury St. Edmunds, Suffolk
Printed and bound in Great Britain by
T. J. Press (Padstow) Ltd., Padstow, Cornwall

**To Rhoda
for
her help**

1

ROSS MACALLISTER eased the little Triumph Herald into a narrow space between two parked cars; he smiled fleetingly at Maureen, his wife, then switched off the engine.

"Made it!" He withdrew the ignition keys. "Never thought I'd find a parking space so near the middle of York! What's next on the day's agenda?"

She looked at the shopping list in her hands. "I'll do the heavy stuff first," she told him. "The new curtains for the lounge and my new coat. I can get them nearby and bring them back to the car . . . then the groceries . . ."

"What about lunch?"

"That snack bar near The Shambles. I like it there. Look, Ross. I know you hate shopping. Why don't you have a browse round your bookshops and meet me before lunch? Say the top of The Shambles?"

"All right. I'll do my bits and pieces, then we can finish the shopping after we've eaten. Meet you at twelve-thirty then!"

"And not a minute later!" She shook a finger at him. "It's quarter to eleven now—that gives me plenty of time."

"So long as you don't spend too much of my hard-earned cash!" He leaned across and kissed her on the cheek. The sunshine of late autumn caressed her deep auburn hair for a passing second, then vanished behind a cloud. "Come along, old girl," he said, "let's get cracking!"

He climbed out and Maureen grabbed a shopping bag; then having locked the doors, they walked along the Market Place, cutting through the narrow streets to the top of The Shambles. This was York's quaintest street, narrow and steeped in history, yet still a busy thoroughfare.

"The parting of the ways," he said.

"I'll pop in here, then I'll see you at this very spot, at twelve-thirty!"

"Mind you do!" Maureen turned away from him and was soon lost in the crowds of this busy Thursday morning.

Ross waited a moment or two, savouring the atmosphere of old York, and turned into the bookshop which stood at the entrance to this famous olde worlde street. He squeezed his way into the tiny, musty interior, past the racks of paperbacks and into the depths of the shop, where he began to examine the novels and works of reference.

Time passed quickly; Ross MacAllister was enjoying a day free from his job of selling office requisites. In this shop, he was in a dream world, flicking through the pages, enjoying the touch of the bound volumes, the glossy covers, the weight of a book in his strong hands. Eventually a girl assistant approached him.

"Can I help you?"

"Just browsing," he replied. "Killing

time while my wife spends all my money!"

"Poor you!" she rejoined with mock horror at his predicament. "Is there any author who interests you particularly? If your book is not in stock we can get it for you."

"I'll make do with a paperback," he said. "Got anything about race relations?"

"There's a Pelican about the Race War," she told him, "on the stands near the door."

"Thanks. I'll invest in a copy." He moved away.

Ten minutes later, he was striding across the Market Square, with the book tucked in his pocket. He was heading for the bridge across the Ouse for there was a musty little bookshop at the other side. It specialized in old books, particularly leatherbound editions—he might find a bargain.

Somewhere above him, a clock struck twelve, slowly and ponderously calling out the strokes, one by one. He found himself counting the heavy notes of the bell.

"Twelve!" He strode on. "Half an hour to go. Just nice time." Maureen would be late anyway. She always was. When she got her nose into a shopping centre, time meant nothing. He poked and peered among the dusty shelves, bringing out volume after volume, and replacing them. There was nothing this week—nothing appealed to him so he glanced at his watch to check on his time. Twenty-five past twelve.

"I'll show her!" he chuckled to himself as he left the shop and turned towards the Bridge for the return journey. Five minutes—he'd show Maureen whether he could keep good time!

As he walked a cool breeze blew from the river, hard and cold against his cheeks, bringing with it a hint of winter. He bowed his head to find shelter from its bite, yet it brought tears to his eyes. In his hazy view, the river beneath had become grey and choppy—the herald of a storm.

He increased his pace; black clouds had replaced the grey ones of an hour ago. They stretched across the sky to his right, ominous and dark. People began to scurry along; office workers trotted with what dignity they could muster, heading for home and a hot lunch during their statutory break of one hour. Shoppers sought shelter in large stores, restaurants and their cars.

Ross's intended destination was the bookshop at the corner of The Shambles; Maureen would look there for him—she may even be there now. He glanced at the threatening clouds; the wind was fresh and cold on his face. The harbinger of rain; heavy rain.

"I'll make it." He gritted his teeth and pulled his sports jacket tight about himself, raising its collar.

He was almost across the bridge, almost clear of the river and its unwelcome wind. Now he could find shelter among the buildings of the city, in the shops and cafés, pubs and alleys.

Ahead of him was a man in a dark suit;

a grey haired gentleman of dignified appearance whose tall, straight figure was not panicked into haste by the threatening storm. He strode purposefully on, with a long and measured stride. A solicitor, perhaps. A barrister. Perhaps an important person from a rich company. A man in authority who felt it beneath him to run or hurry just because everyone else felt it necessary, for there was no rain. Not yet.

Then a splash on Ross's cheek. Automatically, he glanced at the sky to see blackness above him, and to his right there was a downpour sweeping across the city towards him.

The man ahead looked up too; he pulled his jacket high on his shoulders and increased his pace. Ross was ten strides behind him, gaining, starting to run.

The single raindrop had already multiplied into hundreds, heavy and cold. People were scurrying for shelter at each end of the exposed bridge.

Then a car.

It was coming from behind Ross, with screeching gears and the heavy throb of a hard-pressed engine. He turned, frightened by the harsh noise. A drunk was at the wheel. A car out of control. Then it was past him. Two men inside. The driver jerked the steering wheel to his left. Still the accelerator raced the engine. The car mounted the footpath with a crash of metal; it rocked violently, then drove straight at the hurrying man in front of Ross.

"Look out!" cried Ross MacAllister. "Look out."

The man turned. He was pale with a neat moustache. Panic showed for a moment, stark across his handsome features. A thud as the car rammed him, then he was falling.

"Oh God!" breathed Ross. He ran. But the car was leaving. It was hurtling away into the city, engine revving and blood staining its nearside wing and bumper bar. A man's life-blood!

"Stop! You swines, stop!" cried Ross,

with little hope. Clearly they had no intention of stopping.

The car roared away, but not before Ross took its number. ODN 223 X. A Ford Escort—dark green. Two men. Young. That was all he saw. Then there were people, running, shouting, screaming. Panic.

People looked. People stared and people ran away from the rain. Some stopped and looked down at the man, but did no more. Ross bent to examine him, stepping over the blood which poured from a gaping wound in his neck, and from somewhere beneath the man's smart clothes.

"I'll get an ambulance," cried a girl of about eighteen and she ran towards a shop.

Then the rains came down. The heavens burst. Cold, piercing droplets, stinging from the sky, washing away the blood, running down the dying man's face and dripping from his closed eyes. Saturating Ross MacAllister as he held the injured victim in his arms.

The man groaned softly in God-sent unconsciousness; a leg looked awkwardly twisted.

"Police!" shouted Ross to anyone who cared to listen. "Get the police. Is anyone a doctor?"

No one was a doctor. Somebody ran away to telephone for a policeman.

Ross tried to stem the bleeding, but it spurted thick and red from the gaping wound, and the downpour cleaned it away. The rain was running down Ross's neck, down to his vest and pants, down to his socks. Cold and awful.

It soaked the man too. It wiped away the perspiration of shock from his brow. It swilled his life-blood down a drain in the roadside, in moments to seep into the greyness of the River Ouse there to diminish into nothing. A man's life, draining into a river.

But the bleeding wouldn't stop; an artery had been severed by a sharp edge of the murderous car and Ross's efforts, by using his fingers against the man's bones, had little effect.

"Where's the ambulance?" he yelled. "Has someone told them?"

A girl shouted at him, "It's coming . . . I rang from the shop."

A policeman arrived, running through the rain. He was dressed in traffic point gear.

He looked at Ross, hair sodden and clinging to his face. Then he bent to aid the injured man.

"Ambulance?"

"Coming," said Ross.

"Car?"

"Didn't stop."

"See it?"

"Everything."

"Take its number?"

"Of course."

"Thank God for some witnesses! OK. We'll need you. We'll circulate particulars in a minute or two. Must see to this poor soul first. Ah! The ambulance! It's here."

With its blue revolving light piercing the falling rain, a York City ambulance roared towards them and eased to a standstill only a stride from the fallen man.

In a matter of seconds, it was all over. There remained only the blood on the footpath and that was washing away, inch by inch, by the continuing downpour.

"Give me the number, sir. I'll have the swine stopped."

"ODN 223 X—a dark green Ford Escort."

The policeman dragged a personal radio from his pocket and spoke into it. "929—accident on the bridge. A dark green Ford Escort, Number ODN 223 X involved and did not stop. Please trace. Over."

"Thanks," said Ross.

"He'll not get far. Our lads are as keen as mustard. Now, I must take measurements. Can you help me? I'll need you at the office anyhow, to make your statement."

"Sure," said Ross. He helped the policeman to measure the scene—the width of the road, the point of impact from a lamp post . . . the siting of the blood marks. It took only a minute or two, and a clock struck quarter to one.

Five minutes later they walked into York's red brick police office and the policeman shouted to an office man, "Found that car yet?"

"Not a sign, Bill."

"They will. Right. Mr. . . . er . . ."

"MacAllister."

"Mr. MacAllister. Right, come along upstairs, and I'll find some dry clothing for you. I can only offer Civil Defence overalls."

"They'll be fine. Can I make my statement first? I'd like to tell you what happened straightaway. How is the man? Does anyone know?"

"I'll ring the hospital in a minute. Now, this is the interview room. Had your lunch?"

"No, but meals can wait for a thing like this . . ."

"Mine can't. I'll bring some from the canteen . . . we'll eat while we talk."

"But . . ."

"Look, Mr. MacAllister. There's nothing we can do. Every policeman for miles around knows that car number now.

The victim is in hospital where he's getting every attention, so where's the panic?"

"I suppose you're right. . . . OK. I'll have something to eat."

"Then get changed first . . ."

"OK . . . Crikey! My wife! I arranged to meet her . . ."

"Where? When?"

"Top of The Shambles—half-past twelve."

"I'll tell a cadet to telephone the café in the Market Place . . . they'll pass a message to her. What's she look like?"

Ross explained and suggested Maureen be told to get her lunch—he'd see her in an hour or so.

The gruff, but helpful policeman vanished as Ross squelched across the floor of the interview room to a hard chair before a table.

Three minutes later, the constable was back with two hot canteen meals on a tray and a pair of blue overalls and a roller towel dangling from his arm.

"Change here if you like," he said,

tossing the overalls and towel to Ross. "Then tell me the story as we eat. I'll take it down in statement form when we've had our food."

As the policeman tucked into his meal, Ross dried himself vigorously and quickly changed into the makeshift clothes. Then he began to eat.

"Well?"

"There's one thing I must say," said Ross, "but it's only an opinion."

"Go on."

"I think it was deliberate."

The policeman stopped eating.

"No! Lost control, hit the chap and panicked. Daren't face the music. We get dozens like that. Usually, though, they're not so serious."

"It *was* deliberate," emphasized Ross. "I know it was."

"Attempted murder?"

"What else."

The constable munched his Yorkshire pudding, thinking hard. "You'd never convince a court, you know. Hit-and-run accident. Nothing more."

"It was a deliberate attempt to kill that man. I'll put that in my statement."

"Well, you saw it, Mr. MacAllister. Tell me more, and before I write down your statement, I'll fetch our Detective Inspector. We'll see what he thinks of your story."

Ross was enjoying the meal, in spite of the scene that was repeating itself in his mind. He saw it again and again, it was deliberate. It couldn't be anything else.

Then the telephone rang on the window ledge of the room and the constable answered it.

"Watkins," he said. He listened. Then he replaced the receiver and turned to Ross.

"He's dead!" was all he said.

2

"I'M not surprised," Ross commented, "he'd had a shocking knock. Who is he?"

"Dunno yet. I'll have to go to the hospital next. Now, I'll ring Inspector Thomas."

"Gwyn Thomas?"

"Know him?"

"He's a close friend—I'll explain my theory to him. . . ."

"Tell you what then—he'll take a statement from you if you ask him, then I can get along to the hospital. There'll be a post mortem to fix up, and relatives to find."

"And the car that killed him!" put in Ross for good measure.

"We'll find that all right," and this policeman, PC Watkins, picked up the telephone. "Put me through to the canteen, will you? I want Inspector Thomas."

In a moment, he was speaking to Inspector Gwyn Thomas.

"Watkins, sir, in the interview room. I've got a Mr. Ross MacAllister here—he witnessed a fatal hit-and-run a few minutes ago. He'd like a word with you about it."

Gwyn Thomas must have replied in the affirmative, because Watkins said, "I'll tell him, sir."

After replacing the receiver, Watkins turned to Ross and said, "He's finishing his rice pudding. Be down in a second. Have I got your address? We'll want you as a witness at the inquest."

"Ross MacAllister, Briar Cottage, Ryethorpe. Phone number is Ryethorpe 222 if you need that."

The policeman jotted them down. "You're a valuable witness to us, Mr. MacAllister."

"Don't worry!" grinned MacAllister. "I'll come to the inquest. I'm not worried about that sort of thing."

"Good." Then the door opened. "Ah, you're here, sir."

And Gwyn Thomas strode in, pipe in his mouth and a grin of welcome on his handsome face. He was dressed in casual tweeds with brown brogue shoes—a smart and well-groomed Detective Inspector.

"Nice to see you, Ross. But if you're here, there'll be trouble!"

"Now don't be like that, Gwyn!" They shook hands.

Gwyn Thomas settled himself on a chair beside the table, and looked up at PC Watkins.

"What happened, Watkins?"

"Hit-and-run, on the bridge, sir. Chap walking along the footpath towards the City centre, and a car mounted the pavement and mowed him down. He died in hospital. The car didn't stop."

"Any witnesses?"

Ross spoke, "Just me, Gwyn. I got the number—nearly got killed too. I was only a few yards behind the deceased fellow. Bloody horrible, it was."

"Number circulated? Descriptions?"

"All done, sir," replied PC Watkins. "I

was about to take a statement from Mr. MacAllister. Er, he has a theory, sir."

Gwyn Thomas removed his pipe and looked slyly across at his friend. There was a twinkle in his eye. . . .

"You bloody well would have a theory, Ross. You read all kinds of mysteries into everything that happens."

"Now you know damned well you're exaggerating, Gwyn! And it's not often I'm wrong!"

"All right. Spill the beans, my boy." And his Welsh accent sounded alien against the Yorkshire background.

"I think it was deliberate, Gwyn. I think it was a deliberate attempt to run down that man."

Gwyn Thomas sighed heavily. "No, Ross. I can't swallow that one. A murder attempt, you're trying to say? In the middle of a busy city in broad daylight?"

"Why not, Gwyn? Why not? Tell me that!"

"But this sort of thing doesn't happen! A hit-and-run accident? We get dozens of them—there'd be some unknown reason for swerving off the road."

"That car was *driven* at the kerb edge. It came directly at it, from somewhere behind me. I heard it. I saw it. It was *driven* at that man, Gwyn. I saw the bloody thing. I saw the expressions on the occupants' faces, Gwyn; that was a cold blooded murder, if anything was."

"Any other witnesses, Watkins?" asked Gwyn Thomas.

"Not to my knowledge, sir. We might get some if we give the accident sufficient publicity."

"I think we should try everything in view of what Ross thinks—even radio and TV."

"Then you believe me?"

"I didn't say that, Ross! We'll need a statement from you, so you can explain your theories in that."

"PC Watkins did tell me. Can you take it down, Gwyn? He wants to get down to the hospital to see about the dead man."

"For you, yes. OK, Watkins. Get a cadet to bring me some statement forms, will you? Then you get down to the hospital."

"Sir," said PC Watkins.

"Right," said Gwyn Thomas, "tell me what happened, Ross. Every detail—including the rain! I see you're modelling some of our latest Civil Defence overalls!"

"My clothes need drying."

"I'll have them taken to the Fire Brigade's drying room. It'll take hours to get them properly dry."

"I can call back. Right. Now, this is what happened. I was walking across the bridge, into town . . ."

At the hospital, the body of the deceased —a man about fifty—had been removed from the bed it occupied and was now in the hospital mortuary, lying on a cold stone slab. It was dressed in a long white shroud. The clothes and belongings had been placed in a basket on a corner table.

The hospital staff knew the routine when a body was the subject of police enquiries, and so they would leave it well alone until the police had done everything they required. They knew that someone would be coming shortly.

That person arrived in the shape of PC Watkins who was shown to the clinically fresh mortuary, white tiled and smelling strongly of disinfectant. The mortuary attendant accompanied him—a sombre man, with thick yellow teeth and grey eyes which seldom smiled. He was a man accustomed to death in all its forms, sad or sudden, violent or gentle.

Without a word, he moved to the slab and pulled back the sheet.

"That's the chap," said PC Watkins, pulling out his notebook. He then took down a description of the wounds—a lacerated neck, severe bruising to the body, and a deep gash across the back.

"Fractured ribs and a broken spinal column too, mate. Felt him give as I laid him out."

"Poor devil. I'll have to wait until the pathologist finds those injuries before I can officially record them."

"I'm right."

"I'm sure you are, George. But I've got to do things officially. Now, who is he?"

"Clothes over there."

PC Watkins picked up the jacket and began to search its pockets.

He listed the items and put them on a table, one by one.

"Handkerchief, white; Ball point pen, blue; ah, wallet, brown leather, fold-over type."

He opened it.

"Good God!"

"What's up?" asked George, the mortuary attendant.

"Money! Stacks of it! In fivers!"

George came across to have a look. He whistled. "Phew! How much?"

PC Watkins was counting the money.

"Two hundred and fifty," he said. "Hell of a lot to carry about! Make a note of that, George. I don't want anybody thinking I've nicked any. Now, what else is there?"

He found two pound notes and a ten shilling note tucked into another compartment and a small white card with "Mrs.

Hannah Dowd, 42 Albany Crescent, Edgbaston, Birmingham 15".

"A name and address. That's a start."

But that was all. Nothing else.

Who was Mrs. Dowd? His wife? She would have to be interviewed and told of his death. He continued to look through the pockets, but found nothing else, so turned to the trousers. These revealed only the usual bits and pieces carried by a man—a comb, another handkerchief (used), eight and fourpence in cash, a pocket knife, a Yale key No. 486772.

"That all, Mr. Watkins?"

"That's all, George. No name. That's bloody funny to say the least, especially for a chap like him. Looks quite posh and businesslike, doesn't he?"

"Clean too. Nicely washed; well kept sort of chap. Look at his hands. Not a manual worker, is he?"

"Fingerprints!" realized PC Watkins. "Looks as though we might have trouble getting him identified, unless this Dowd woman can help. I'll want his prints. And a detailed description to circulate to other forces. Clothes too. Forensic chaps might want a look at them. Now, I'll have to fix a post mortem. Who's your new pathologist?"

"Doctor Anthony Woodford. Started last week after old Brotherton retired. Not a bad chap."

"Will he be in his office?"

"Sure."

"Good. I'll have a word with him now, then ring the Coroner to make it all official. Then I'll have to get down to finding out who this chap is."

In the meantime, Ross MacAllister had dictated his statement to his friend, Inspector Thomas, who had taken it down in longhand. In accordance with police procedure, he read it over to Ross.

"You insist on putting in your opinion that it was deliberate?"

"I do, Gwyn. It's important."

"I agree, but damned hard to prove. Anyway, it's your statement. Sign the bottom please, then you can go."

"I must get cracking. Maureen will be doing her nut!"

"She's used to it, surely? Nothing you do is ever straightforward."

Ross grinned. "She'll understand," he said simply.

"What about your clothes? They won't be dry yet."

"Can I go in these overalls? If you run me to my car . . ."

"If you think I've got time to run a taxi service for the benefit of Ross MacAllister . . ."

"Aw, come on, Gwyn! You can call it 'Enquiries'—drop me off at the car park and I'll drive home in the overalls. I can call back tomorrow for my jacket and things."

"All right. Come along. I'll leave these statements in the office—the Coroner will want a copy today."

"Can we see if they've traced that car yet?"

"Sure."

But they hadn't. There had been absolutely no word, except a telephone call from the hospital to say that PC Watkins was staying there awhile because the Coroner had ordered a post mortem, and Doctor Woodford said he'd do it immediately. Watkins had, therefore, telephoned a verbal description of the man, his clothing and the little printed card to the office, where the necessary enquiries would be initiated. The Photographic Department was requested to fingerprint the body and to take photographs of the corpse for any future circulation.

And so the wheels of police machinery began to turn. The incident had come to the notice of local journalists who simply recorded it in the Evening Press as a road accident. They were told no more at that stage.

In the meantime, the rain had ceased, Gwyn Thomas had dropped Ross off at his car in York Market Place and he sat there alone, waiting for Maureen. Gwyn had gone back via The Shambles hoping to catch Maureen near the bookshop. But he must have missed her. Fifteen minutes elapsed and Ross began to feel chilly.

"Come on, Maureen..." he was saying, "hurry up!"

Maureen had seen Gwyn Thomas's car drive past the little restaurant where she was enjoying a coffee after her lunch and she rushed out in time to see him vanish round a corner.

She had received the message about Ross, so was Gwyn looking for her with more news?

She dithered slightly, then returned to settle her bill before leaving.

She would return to their car. That's it. Ross might be there.

As she hurried to the park she sighed ... life with Ross MacAllister was never dull, never placid and organized, never predictable.

He had served his National Service in the Royal Air Force before marrying Maureen, and there he'd found excitement as a navigator with a bomber crew. His service missions had taken him to Suez, to Kenya and to various Middle East stations, and she knew he'd done secret work in connection with his flights. In fact, he'd been recalled once or twice to undertake further missions for the Air Force. But he didn't talk about them—there was a hint of espionage though.

But now that he was married with a family, Ross didn't particularly yearn for excitement, and so he'd bought a cottage in Ryethorpe and had taken a quiet sort of job—he was a salesman for Messrs. Tombridges and Company, a wholesale Office Requisites firm who sold to the trade. His territory was the North East of England, from the Humber to the Tyne and for a time he'd found that his leisure periods allowed him to pursue his hobbies. He liked to roam around the countryside and examine quaint villages and old inns. He liked the thrill of motor rallying with his pals and he enjoyed shooting competitions against neighbouring rifle clubs. He was his club's pistol shooting champion this year—for his sport, he had bought a match pistol which he kept at home. He'd been granted a Firearms Certificate to make the whole thing legal.

But as Maureen had discovered, Ross had an uncanny knack of getting involved in criminal escapades, and because of this he had become acquainted with Detective Inspector Gwyn Thomas of the local force. Their frequent meetings had developed into a very close friendship.

But things had reached a stage where Maureen hardly dare let Ross out of the house! So what had happened now? She hurried to the car and pushing through the shoppers, saw him sitting there, calm and patient.

She decreased her urgent pace; he was there as large as life, as if nothing had happened.

"Ah, there you are," he beamed through the open window. "You didn't get wet then?"

"Ross!" she shrieked as she saw the overalls, "what happened?"

"I got caught in that downpour," he said calmly. "Hop in and I'll tell you all about it."

"But you've been to the police station," she was moving to her own side of the car, "they rang me at the café."

"It was nothing," he said. "I witnessed an accident and they wanted a statement from me."

"When?"

"Half-past twelve. I was coming to meet you—bang on time, too—when a car knocked a chap down on the bridge. It didn't stop, and I happened to see the whole affair. I did what I could for the poor chap who'd been bumped and got soaked in the process. And that's all."

"Is it? Is it as simple as that, Ross?" Maureen was now settled in the passenger seat, looking earnestly at her husband.

"He's dead. The pedestrian died."

"Go on," she said, knowing Ross's mannerism. His hesitant speech, his sidewards glances told her there was more.

"Nothing else."

"I don't believe you, but come along. Let's go home. Jennifer and Paul will be coming home from school soon, and I told Mrs. Potter we'd collect Clare and Baby

Timothy at three o'clock. We're always late when she's baby sitting. . . ."

"She doesn't mind. She loves children," and he started the car.

After tea, Ross helped Maureen to wash the dishes, then he settled down to watch the news on Yorkshire Television.

"Maureen," he called through to the kitchen, "that accident might be mentioned—they talked of a TV appeal for witnesses."

She came through and watched in silence as the programme preceding the news came to an end. Then the commercials flashed their merry way across the screen, to conclude with a stark legend "Police Message".

"Here we are," cried Ross, "listen."

The announcer spoke, unseen.

"Here is a Police Message," he began. "At twelve-thirty this afternoon, an accident occurred in The Headrow, Leeds, when a man was knocked down by a motor car which failed to stop. The man has since died. Will anyone who witnessed the accident, or who can give any information, please contact Leeds City Police, or any police officer."

"You said it happened in York!" snapped Maureen in disbelief.

"It did," said Ross. "At half-past twelve! Give me the phone!"

"No, Ross. Please don't get involved. It's a coincidence. . . . It must be."

But Ross MacAllister was already dialling for Inspector Gwyn Thomas.

3

"BUT it's worth checking with Leeds, Gwyn," persisted Ross. "I knew it might be a coincidence, but both at the same time, both hit-and-runs. It stinks to me."

"I'll ring them and get details, if that will keep you quiet!"

"You'll ring back?"

"Of course."

"Who's our deceased chap, Gwyn?"

"We don't know, Ross. No papers on him, except a printed visiting card, with a Birmingham address. We're checking down there, but haven't had a reply."

"Funny."

"Not especially. Men do go around with nothing in their pockets to identify them. I've done it myself."

"I thought you were having a TV appeal too."

"We did. On BBC One."

"Oh! Any results?"

"Not a bloody sausage, Ross. He might be a local man, you know—the fact he had no documents rather suggests that."

"It's possible—any sign of the car yet? It's strange that it hasn't been traced?"

"I agree, but these things take time. We've checked the number you gave us, Ross. It's a York registration."

"And?"

"And it's false...."

"False!" shrieked Ross. "Then I was right! It was a deliberate attempt!"

"Hold it, Ross!"

"But if they used a car with false plates on it..."

"If they used a car with false plates on it, it might have been stolen and driven by someone who couldn't control it. The person who knocked down our unknown man might be an unlicensed person who panicked and cleared off."

"You talk too much like a policeman, Gwyn!"

"That's because I am a policeman! I must maintain an open mind on such matters. Anyway, thanks for the tip about the Leeds accident. I'll ring straight away. By the way, I've been to the drying room in the Fire Station—your clothes are ready to collect any time—dry as dust now."

"I might be in York tomorrow, Gwyn."

"Good. Pop in for a coffee if you've time and I'll keep you up to date with any developments."

"Right. Now, let me settle down—it's Top of the Pops on BBC One tonight."

"Do you watch that?" There was genuine surprise and even horror in Gwyn Thomas's voice.

"Without fail, Gwyn, my friend. Keeps me young, you know! When you're topping thirty like me, you've got to keep up with modern trends."

"Can't say I follow your reasoning, Ross. Anyway, must go: I'll call back in a few moments."

At ten to six that same evening, Police Constable Rodney Hughes paraded for duty at York police station for his eight hour stint until two o'clock in the morning. He read the events of the day in the Occurrence Book, and noted the message about the green Ford with its false number plates. He also read and noted the *Police Gazette*, the West Riding Police Reports and his local force's crime circulations.

On the stroke of six, Rodney Hughes, feeling thoroughly competent with five years' police service, strode into the city with a determination to check every car park for the green Ford Escort. Furthermore, he would check every possible hiding place, for the city was full of such corners and alleys where stolen cars, motor cycles and courting couples hid themselves away from prying eyes. But seldom did such things or persons conceal themselves from Rodney Hughes. He was a man who could find the tiniest needle in the largest haystack.

He set to work. If that car was in York, Rodney Hughes would find it.

He did.

He found it tucked away in a lonely

scrap yard on the outskirts, driven well behind a pile of rusting scrap iron and household junk; only the rear portion showed, but it didn't escape the eagle eyes of Rodney Hughes.

He knew this yard—it belonged to Amos Adams and he used it as a dumping ground for all manner of scrap. Lorry loads came and went; the vehicles rarely stayed here for more than a few minutes and so the place didn't carry any resident workers. That explained why the car hadn't been noticed before.

Rodney approached with great caution; the Ford still bore false number plates and was clearly abandoned.

There was no sign of anyone in the vehicle, so Rodney Hughes moved in close, still wary and ready for anything. His young heart thumped with intense excitement as he peered through the back window. Empty. Keys still in the ignition.

Next he walked around to examine the front nearside of the car—the message in the Occurrence Book said the car involved in the accident would be damaged on the front nearside after running down the pedestrian. And PC Hughes found blood on the metalwork. The front headlamp glass was also smashed and the jagged pieces which remained were spattered with deep red blood. So was the end of the bumper bar.

Hughes didn't touch anything; he simply spoke into his pocket radio and asked for the CID.

They came and thoroughly examined the car, seeking fingerprints and other identifying features, but they drew a blank. Furthermore, when the false number plates were removed, it was found that the real ones had also been taken away and the taxation disc was missing. The owner of the car could not be readily traced.

"Do we know of any dark green Ford Escorts stolen recently?" asked Rodney Hughes.

The detective sergeant in charge of the operation shook his head. "Nope. Nothing stolen locally."

"Can we check by its engine number?"

"Possibly. I'll have it towed to the station now; we can't do any more here, and we'll circulate the engine and chassis numbers. Might come up with something. This scrap yard belongs to old Adams, doesn't it?"

"Yes."

"Right. Pop round and see him, Rodney. Find out if any of his men have been here today—someone might have seen the Ford driven in."

"Right, Sergeant. Anything else to do here?"

"No, lad. And well done—if you keep up this sort of work, we'll find a vacancy for you in plain clothes."

"I'd like that, Sergeant."

And PC Rodney Hughes went on his way, happy and contented.

He would put his heart into this enquiry.

Twenty miles away, in the heart of Leeds, a dead man lay in a mortuary, and

Detective Sergeant Kilby stood by the body, chatting to the pathologist.

"I'm afraid we haven't identified him yet, doctor. He had very little with him—a wallet with a few pounds, but no documents."

"And the car which hit him?"

"A woman with a baby saw the accident and she described the car as a pale colour, possibly fawn, but she couldn't guess the make. Modern looking, by all accounts, though. It mounted a traffic island where the deceased was standing at the time; mowed him down and careered off into the traffic without stopping."

"The swines!"

"There might have been two people in the car—the woman thinks it contained a man and a woman, but can't be sure. She didn't see the number."

"Youngsters joyriding, more than likely. Panicked as the car got out of control. They'll have dumped it by now."

"Almost certainly, doctor. Every policeman in Leeds is looking for the vehicle."

"Well, Sergeant, your man died from multiple injuries and shock as a direct result of the accident. They made a real job of it."

"The witness said something odd, you know, doctor. She said, 'I thought it was deliberate. It drove on to the island straight at him.'"

"Imagination on her part, perhaps, but worth keeping in mind, Sergeant."

"We've put a TV appeal out for witnesses, but nothing's come in yet."

"Good. Well, I'll write out my report and let you have a copy for the Coroner," concluded the pathologist.

Detective Sergeant Kilby left the mortuary and drove back to Leeds City Police Headquarters to record his attendance at the post mortem, and to write up his notebook.

For him, this wasn't a particularly exciting duty; he'd been in the office, about to go for lunch, when a report had arrived of a man being knocked down in the Headrow by a car which failed to stop. Hit-and-run accidents were a common occurrence in any police area, although fatalities which occurred in this manner weren't particularly commonplace.

The Superintendent had sent Kilby out to supervise a young police constable who was dealing with the accident, but the thing had snowballed until Sergeant Kilby found himself taking over.

At first, this had upset him—hit-and-run accidents weren't within the normal scope of detective sergeants' duties, and when he had made his little protest, the Superintendent had said, "Jump to it, Sergeant—you're still a policeman even though you're in plain clothes. Won't do you any harm!"

And so he had undertaken this duty; and as he performed his various tasks the words of the woman witness echoed in his mind, "I thought it was deliberate . . . I thought it was deliberate . . ."

He settled at his desk to begin his report and the telephone rang.

"Sergeant Kilby."

It was the relief operator on the

exchange. "I've a call from York, Sergeant. A Detective Inspector wants to talk to you about that hit-and-run."

"Put him through."

In a moment, they were connected and Sergeant Kilby said, "Detective Sergeant Kilby speaking."

"Detective Inspector Thomas, York. Are you dealing with that hit-and-run?"

"Yes, sir. Nasty business." Kilby heard the distinct Welsh accent across the telephone. "You've heard about it then?"

"Your bit on TV—we had a similar appeal at the same time on the other channel!"

"You've had a hit-and-run too, sir?"

"Yes. And both have similarities. Ours occurred at twelve-thirty this afternoon, just like yours; our car mounted a footpath and the dead man is, at the moment, unidentified. I felt I must ring you about the two accidents—it does seem a little strange."

Sergeant Kilby's ears pricked up at this; it might prove an opportunity to hit back at the Superintendent who gave him this onerous duty. If only he could prove a criminal link-up. . . .

"In our case, sir," Kilby was saying, "the car mounted a traffic island in the Headrow and killed a man. Our man is unknown too."

"What sort of a car?"

"We don't know. Fawn colour or some other light shade. That's all we have. We haven't traced it yet."

"We've got ours—a dark green Ford Escort with false plates. It was stolen."

"So the only similarities are the time the accidents occurred, and the fact that each dead man is unknown."

"Both vehicles failed to stop, remember. If yours is abandoned somewhere, we may find another link."

"Possibly, sir. As a matter-of-fact, there is something else—a woman who witnessed the Leeds accident thought it was a deliberate attempt to run down the man. Her exact words were, 'I thought it was deliberate—it drove on to the island straight at him'."

At the far end of the telephone link,

Gwyn Thomas whistled. "Really? Well we have a witness—a good one too—who said exactly the same about the York accident. . . ."

Kilby felt a surge of excitement in his veins; this was no ordinary hit-and-run. Here was a chance to make a name for himself.

"It looks curious, sir. Anything I can do?"

"Send me a full report of your accident, will you? Photographs of the deceased, fingerprints—the lot. A photograph of the scene might not be a bad idea either. Anything you can give."

"You'll do the same for me?"

"Of course. We'll keep in touch to see if there are other similarities. You say you haven't traced the car yet?"

"No. But I'll make sure the beat men give the car parks and waste ground a thorough going-over tonight. I'll pull out every stop to find that car."

"We found ours in York City."

"Thanks. Any other leads, sir?"

"Not at this stage, Sergeant. I just

wanted a chat to establish a few more facts—now that I am fairly confident there is a connection, I suggest we concentrate on identifying our victims."

"That's my next job," said Sergeant Kilby.

"Then I'll let you get on with it, Sergeant. Good-bye."

"'Bye, sir."

Detective Sergeant Kilby replaced the telephone and attacked his report with a new interest. He might get himself a Chief Constable's commendation if he sorted out this little lot—he wouldn't tell anyone about the York connection—not yet. This was his trump card.

Back in York, Gwyn Thomas put down his telephone and looked at his watch. It was well past tea time. But still time to ring Ross MacAllister before leaving. He asked the operator to get him Ryethorpe 222, and in five minutes was talking to Ross MacAllister.

"Just going home for tea, Ross, and thought I'd let you know the latest. We've found the car you saw—it has false plates, and I've had words with Leeds about their accident. It was just like ours, almost a carbon copy. Even their victim is unknown."

"Then you are treating it as murder?"

"Not yet—we haven't enough proof."

"I see your point. OK. Thanks for ringing, Gwyn. I'll pop in to see you tomorrow."

In Birmingham, Detective Constable Barry Waterford parked in Albany Crescent and walked along the row of Georgian houses, seeking number forty-two.

His enquiry was simple—he had to learn the name of a man killed in York in a road accident, and he had a brief description of the man.

York police had told him that a Mrs. Hannah Dowd lived at number forty-two. The dead man had her visiting card in his pocket, so the enquiry would be straightforward.

He found the house. It had a large

ornate door with pillars at each side, and a gold number "42" in the glass above. He climbed the steps and rang the door bell.

It echoed inside the rambling house and he waited.

No reply.

They said the enquiry was urgent, so he rang again. It was loud enough—you could hear it in the street, and he tried the knob. The door swung open easily.

"Mrs. Dowd?"

No reply.

"Mrs. Dowd? You there?"

He stepped into the large entrance hall, carpeted with a long clean, but shabby carpet, and made for the kitchen. These houses were all the same, with a kitchen at the distant end, large and airy.

"Mrs. Dowd," he called, and he pushed open the kitchen door.

Horror met him; stark, unreal horror, for there was a woman on the floor. Her head and face were battered beyond recognition. That she was dead was beyond all doubt.

"Mrs. Dowd," was all he could say. "Mrs. Dowd."

4

BIRMINGHAM CITY police swung into immediate action and their own murder squad took over number forty-two Albany Crescent to begin a meticulous investigation.

One of the investigating officers rang York to speak with Inspector Gwyn Thomas; he was put through to his home number.

"Detective Sergeant Cawthorne, Birmingham, sir. I believe you asked for enquiries to be made of a Mrs. Dowd of Edgbaston, about a motoring accident."

"Yes, I did. Got some news?"

"She's been found murdered, sir."

"Murdered! Good God!"

"Yes. Our man entered the house upon receiving no response—she's been brutally attacked with some form of blunt instrument—our Superintendent told me to ring you."

"You did right. Hell, this is snowballing . . ." and he explained the situation to the Birmingham sergeant.

"If you can let us have photographs of your victim, sir, we can start enquiries down here. If he did stay with Mrs. Dowd, someone might have seen him."

"I'll send a file. I'll ring Leeds too and ask them to do the same. Their victim might be connected with Mrs. Dowd as well."

"Thank you, sir. Good-bye."

According to the police scientists, Mrs. Dowd had been dead for some eight hours, and had been clubbed to death by a series of savage blows with a blunt instrument. A search of the house failed to trace the weapon, and so a major publicity campaign was launched in an attempt to find it.

There appeared to be no motive. Nothing in the house had been disturbed. A systematic and thorough search of the house revealed nothing which could be connected with her death.

Her attacker may have entered through either the back or front door. Both were unlocked and there were no marks of violence on the premises—no broken windows, or signs of a forcible entry.

The man in charge of the Birmingham operation was Detective Superintendent Hamish Hamilton. He was a burly Scotsman with a flowing orange moustache, fiery and abrupt. He had known the reason for Detective Constable Waterford's visit to this house, and, therefore, sought some evidence of visitors to the house, either friendly or otherwise. If she did take in residents, there should be a boarding house register—every keeper of premises which were used for accommodation was legally bound to maintain a register of guests; he found one. Tattered and old, a simple exercise book tucked in her bureau.

Hamilton took it for further enquiries, and decided he must investigate the past life of Mrs. Hannah Dowd. She was a woman of elderly years—nearing seventy perhaps, certainly over sixty judging by her appearance, and her house indicated that she was a woman who had fought for every penny she earned. A tidy house furnished with poor quality furniture. A widow perhaps?

There were a lot of enquiries to be made, and Hamilton settled down to tabulate the questions to which he must put an answer; around him the routine work of the murder investigation was carried out. Photographs, fingerprints, the detailed and meticulous examination of the scene with every modern scientific aid.

The questions. Already a team of young, enthusiastic detectives were visiting the surrounding houses, gathering facts and gossip about Mrs. Dowd. Very shortly, her most intimate secrets would be recorded in the police files. Nothing would be a secret any longer. Nothing.

That was the one thing that Superintendent Hamilton disliked about a murder enquiry—it revealed everything about the victim but so little about the killer. The mind of the victim could be interpreted and understood, but so rarely was the mind of the killer laid open for analysis.

He stuffed his list of questions deep into his pocket, lit a huge pipe and went to supervise the work in the house.

Ross MacAllister's telephone rang. It was Gwyn Thomas, ringing from home.

"Can you come over, Ross? To the office. We've had a call from Birmingham —that woman whose address we found on the body has also been found murdered. We've started off a right hornet's nest— I want you to come and make an Identikit picture of the men you saw in the killer car."

"I didn't get a very good look at them, Gwyn."

"I know, but any sight is better than none. Clearly we've set off a real hare and I'll have to pull out every stop at my end of the enquiry."

"I'll get off now, Gwyn. See you in half-an-hour or so."

"Well done. I'd value your brain on

this enquiry—I'm running short of ideas and leads now."

"You don't need me! But I'll be glad to help in any way I can."

"Thanks. See you shortly at the office."

Maureen pleaded with Ross to be careful, and he tried to put her mind at ease.

"I'm just going to make an Identikit picture of the men in that car," he told her. "There's no danger in that. And I'll bring my clothes back too."

"You've said that sort of thing before. 'I'm just going to help' you've said, and you've got deeply involved, every time. Don't get involved this time, Ross. Please. By what I hear, these must be ruthless people you're dealing with."

"I'll do my picture, darling, then come straight home. I promise."

He stopped and kissed her full on her lips. She was a beautiful woman; she had exquisite features crowned by a head of gorgeous auburn hair which seemed to catch every glint of light in the room. A true beauty.

"I won't wait up," were her parting words.

"I'll be back before you're in bed!" and he left his cottage. Maureen listened as his Triumph Herald accelerated through the village, its sound dying to nothing as he sped through the lanes.

She turned her attention to the television set, but she couldn't concentrate.

In York Police Office, Ross MacAllister had difficulty in recalling the features of the two men in the killer car. There were two—he could remember that. But they had roared past him in a blur of evil movement; two men. Two nondescripts.

Gwyn Thomas was sitting beside him.

"We'll take the driver first, Ross. Age? Can you estimate his age?"

"You're asking me to put a finger on his age, Gwyn, and I just don't know."

"Was he your age then? Under thirty?"

"Oh, yes. Under thirty."

"Right, then we've started. Now, his hair—fair, dark, brown, thin?"

"Dark. They were both dark, in fact. Longish hair. . . ."

"Straight?"

"No, curly, I'd say. That's it. The driver had curly hair—a thick mop of it."

"Any other hair on his face? Moustache? Beard?"

"I don't think so. I couldn't really see him—he was at the other side of the car. The passenger was nearest me."

"We'll come to him in a minute. Now—glasses? Had the driver glasses?"

"No. Plumpish, though, I'd say he was heavily built with a rounded face."

"Clothes? Anything distinctive about his clothes?"

Ross shook his head. "I can't honestly remember anything about his clothes, Gwyn. Nothing at all."

"All right. We'll leave him for a moment. Now, the passenger. How about him?"

"I saw him fairly well. He was youngish—well below thirty. I'd place him in his middle twenties, and he had sharper features than his mate."

"Hair?"

"Dark like his mate, but it was long and not so curly. It hung down straight —almost like a woman's."

"Anything else about him?"

"He was leaning forward in the seat—the passenger seat at the front—and he was gripping the dashboard. I can see him now. The car was heading straight for that unfortunate man, and this character, the passenger, had his eyes fixed on the target. Bright eyes, unnaturally bright, and a pointed nose. Sallow complexion . . . no specs. And he had a dark brown jacket on; it might have been dark suède, Gwyn. And he had one of those white polo necked shirts on. No tie, of course."

"I thought you couldn't remember much about them?"

"I didn't think I could, Gwyn. Funny how it all comes back once you start thinking."

"Good. Now I want you to keep those pictures in your mind. We'll try to build up a picture on the Identikit. I want you to pay very close attention to the smaller points of each person. Things like the angle of his nose, hairline, shape of ears . . . that sort of thing."

"I've seen this done, Gwyn. It's a wonderful invention."

"Right. Then let's get cracking."

Gradually, the two men built up composite pictures of the men in the green Ford, and all the time Ross corrected and altered the growing pictures; it was amazing how the likenesses grew before them.

Then the telephone rang.

Gwyn Thomas answered it.

"Detective Inspector Thomas, York," he said.

It was Birmingham police.

"Detective Sergeant Cawthorne, Birmingham, sir. We've got some more information for you."

"Excellent. Fire away."

"We've found a notebook in the dead woman's house. It looks like a list of boarders. We're checking up on the names, but we've also found several photographs. Family, mostly."

"What about her husband?"

"He died during the last war. She's a widow, and she never married again."

"Children?"

"Four, we think, judging by some letters we've found. Two sons and two daughters. And that's the point in mind, sir. We have photographs of Mrs. Dowd and her family; it occurred to us that your dead man might be one of her sons."

"Her son! Have you spoken to Leeds about theirs?"

"Not yet. We will ring them next. But my Superintendent felt you ought to see these family photographs and compare them with the body you've got in your morgue."

"I could send pictures...."

"He asked if you could come down to Birmingham, sir. To see things for yourself."

"It's a long way, Sergeant, but at least it would be better if I did make a personal comparison. OK. I'll come immediately; it's nine o'clock now. I can be there shortly after midnight."

"What about the Leeds detectives, sir? I expect they'll be coming too—my boss wants them here as well—for the same reasons."

"I'll ring Leeds if you like," offered Gwyn Thomas. "I can give their man a lift."

"Thank you, sir. We'll expect you when you arrive—we'll be working all night on this case. Probably a damned sight longer by the look of things."

Gwyn Thomas laughed. "Think of your overtime pay, Serge!" then rang off. He turned his attention to Ross. "Got to go, Ross. To Birmingham. There's a possibility that our body is the son of the dead woman in Edgbaston. I'm going over to try to make an identification."

"Can I come?" Ross asked.

"What the hell do you want to come for?" There was genuine surprise in Gwyn Thomas's voice. "You should go home to Maureen!"

"I should, shouldn't I? But you'll be going straight there and back. I'd like to see the set-up in Birmingham.... Maureen won't wait up for me!"

"But you're not a policeman; I don't mind you helping me with my enquiries, but some of these other forces are a bit touchy about outsiders."

"Just there and back, Gwyn. I'll sit in the car all the time if you like. I'm as intrigued as you are about the whole affair."

"It's your decision, Ross. You're welcome to come along with me—in fact, you'll be an asset on a long drive like this. You'll help to keep me awake. Come if you like. Now, I must ring that sergeant at Leeds."

Detective Sergeant Kilby was about to leave his office when Thomas's call came through, and he immediately agreed to join Gwyn Thomas on the trip. Gwyn took the dead man's belongings, including the Yale key, and a file, which included photographs of the corpse.

They left York at nine-thirty; collected Kilby at Leeds shortly before ten-thirty and arrived in Birmingham just after twelve-thirty the following morning, Friday.

Kilby knew the Birmingham area fairly well and guided them to Edgbaston where they asked a night-duty policeman for Albany Crescent.

Number forty-two was ablaze with light; a row of police vehicles was parked outside the house and the building itself was brilliantly lit inside as the intense work of crime detection slowly progressed.

"You'd better wait here, Ross," advised Gwyn Thomas, "until I've had a look around. Come along, Sergeant. Let's see what's happening."

Clutching their files, Inspector Thomas and Sergeant Kilby crossed the wide footpath to mount the steps at the entrance to number forty-two.

Ross watched them go. He sat alone in the York police car and looked at the mass of vehicles around him. Police vehicles of all kinds; photographers' vans, patrol cars, superior officers' cars, even a mobile office.

And bystanders. A little knot of sensation-seekers hovering just along the Crescent, watching the comings and goings. A group of pressmen, cameras popping in the darkness as detectives came and went. Cars slowing down as they passed along the street; occasionally a loud hailer exhorting the public to go home.

Ross waited alone, watching the morbid gathering of people. A little crowd of night wanderers. Lonely people, he guessed. People who knew the unfortunate Mrs. Dowd. Gossips. Neighbours. Friends.

A television camera crew had arrived and were setting up their equipment on the roof of a Land-Rover across the street, filming the events of the night. For some reason, the death of this widow had created undue interest in television and press circles.

A car came up behind Ross and its lights played across the faces of the crowd before him. One by one, the headlights picked out the features, like a stage spotlight picking out the chief actors in a drama.

Ross watched.

"God!" he hissed.

The man at the extreme right! The long straight hair, the pointed nose. The brown jacket. . . .

Waiting in the crowd.

It was the passenger in the deadly Ford! The car that had killed the man in York. The same passenger!

And as Ross watched, the thin faced man began to walk away.

Ross hurried from his car to follow.

5

THE man was tall and slim; he walked quickly with long strides and had his hands tucked into his trousers pockets. He had a slight stooping appearance. As he strode through the wide streets, his long hair moved with the breezes of the night, flowing behind and catching the glints from the street lighting, high above.

The man walked on the outer edge of the pavement, apparently deep in thought; occasionally he stepped on to the road to avoid a street lamp or a pillar box, and Ross had no difficulty in following him.

As Ross tailed him from Albany Crescent, he noted the street names; he noted shops and offices, cross-roads and junctions, so that he could retrace his steps to Gwyn Thomas and his car.

By this time, his quarry had reached a

small knot of brightly lit shops and cafés, where he turned into a snack bar. Ross crossed the road; from there he could watch his prey without being seen, and his dilemma was whether to keep vigil here or return to inform the police of the whereabouts of this character.

In the light of the snack bar, Ross saw the man order a coffee and carry it to a corner table, where he sat and drank it, alone and apparently without concern. He held the mug in both hands, as if warming himself from its heat. He sipped it slowly without glancing about himself. A man with no obvious worries.

"He's not waiting for anyone," thought Ross. "Probably just killing time."

Then the man moved. He drained his mug and left the table; he was clearly outlined in the brilliant lights of the late night snack bar as he turned for the exit. Thin drawn face with hollow cheeks; cheeks which were emphasized by the lights of the snack bar. Staring eyes. The man moved as if he was in a trance.

He emerged and resumed his walk, still

heading away from Albany Crescent, and Ross shadowed him once more. Then, some five minutes later, his quarry disappeared into a public toilet. Ross followed.

As he entered, he heard the clanging of a cubicle door and knew his man had locked himself inside. Ross waited; the only sounds were the hissing of the flushing system and the night traffic outside.

Ten minutes elapsed; the lock was withdrawn and the man emerged; Ross resumed his trail.

His quarry left the main thoroughfare and moved along a dark side street; he walked in the middle of the road, his hands still deep in his pockets. Ross padded along in his wake, but kept to the shadows. There was no indication that the man was aware of Ross's presence, for he continued at a steady, rather fast pace.

Ross was beginning to feel lost; he'd taken a careful note of his route, but now they were in minor streets, dark and sombre. They'd left the main thoroughfares with their sodium lights and shop windows, and were now walking between tall, dark brick built places. Warehouses, stores, the backs of shop premises. Old terraced houses, unoccupied and derelict.

The thin faced youth was forty yards ahead of him, a dark silhouette steadily striding away, and then he stopped abruptly. Ross took two strides, and stopped as well, startled by the sudden alteration in movement.

The man appeared to be listening, but Ross was in the shadows, out of sight. The man moved off again, slowly this time, and occasionally peering over his shoulders.

They were alone in this dark street, this tiny dark alley somewhere in Birmingham; Ross edged forward now, aware that the man was suspicious, or even aware of his follower. But Ross didn't intend losing him at this stage.

Then the long haired character turned to his right, through a door in the wall. It crashed home behind him and he was gone. In the gloom, Ross saw a high wall behind which was a row of terraced houses. This was the back entrance and the houses stood some fifteen yards away. The man would be crossing the dark patch of garden now, heading for the back door of a house.

With every sense alert, Ross crept on silent soles to the door in the wall. He listened. Not a sound. His quarry must have reached the house. With his eyes screwed up against the dim light, Ross MacAllister sought a number on the door, but found nothing. There was no identification of the premises. It was one of a long row of similar doors, and Ross knew he must have some way of knowing it again.

Mark it! He must mark it. A ball point pen! He took one from his pocket and marked the door jamb with his initials, R.M. He scratched them into the paint surface, and knew they could be identified in daylight or by torch.

He listened again. Nothing.

Should he look inside? He ought to see what lay in this garden—perhaps the man was going to bed. More than likely, this was his home.

Ross felt for the door handle; it was an old-fashioned sneck latch and he gripped its handle, then pressed.

The door opened easily; to his relief it didn't squeak. As it opened he saw the large old house in darkness before him. A neglected garden filled the space between himself and the back entrance, and he stepped inside, gently closing the door. He would have a closer look at the house.

A rustle behind him; then blackness. Crashing oblivion. Ross collapsed beneath the blow to his head and rolled over to lie with his face to the stars, utterly unconscious.

Someone lifted his shoulders and dragged him towards the house.

Inside number forty-two Albany Crescent, Gwyn Thomas and Sergeant Kilby were shown to an upstairs room where a gathering of detectives sat around a table.

"Ah, our friends from the frozen north!" grinned a massive man with a deep Scots accent and a huge ginger moustache. "I am Superintendent Hamilton."

"Inspector Thomas," said Gwyn in his Welsh accent, "and this is Sergeant Kilby from Leeds."

"A sergeant? In charge of a murder enquiry?"

Kilby spoke up. "Ours is nothing more than a fatal hit-and-run accident at the moment, sir. It corresponds in many ways to the York accident, so I've come along to see if there is more to it than meets the eye. I just happened to be around when the call came through—otherwise you might have had a raw recruit standing here now!"

"You've got some funny systems in Yorkshire, Sergeant," chuckled Superintendent Hamilton. "However, let's get on with the job. I'm pleased you came—we could have done this by car or post or something, but I like to get on with the job. Now, Inspector Thomas. You saw the body at York?"

"Yes, sir."

"Then I want you to look at these family photographs. See if you can spot your man among them. They were taken some years ago, but you might see a familiar face. Sergeant Kilby—you do likewise please."

Hamilton showed them a pile of photograph albums on a sideboard, plus one or two portraits from various rooms, all brown with age.

"They're a bit ancient, sir," commented Gwyn Thomas.

"Sorry about that. It looks as though she kept a lot of photographs from her young days."

"How old was she?"

"Sixty-five, or thereabouts."

Gwyn continued to look at the family groups as they spoke. "I noticed the TV cameras outside, sir. Why the sudden interest in a murder of this type? They don't usually warrant TV coverage."

"It's not an ordinary murder, Inspector. Mrs. Dowd was once a famous actress. Music hall days, then early films. Stage name of Annette Wallace."

"Annette Wallace! God, I've heard of her!"

"Then she is our victim, Inspector. Hence the press interest. And if the press are interested, it means that our superiors are going to demand results."

"Annette Wallace . . . I've never heard of her for years!"

"She's gone out in a blaze of publicity anyway," grunted the dour Scotsman. "I'll put you in the picture after you've been through those photographs."

Gwyn Thomas and Kilby plodded on with their task, trying to match one of those faces with the corpses in their local mortuaries, but it seemed a hopeless task.

Then Kilby spoke.

"This one, sir. That's like my corpse and it's more recent than the others—quite a modern print. I'm not too sure, mind you, because the fellow in our morgue is going thin on top. This chap has plenty of hair. It makes him look different."

"A wedding group, eh? Best man, isn't he?"

"Yes, standing next to the groom. But even if this is your man, sir, can it help? We don't know who these people are."

"No, but we can find out, Sergeant. If you turn it over," and Kilby did, "you'll see the copyright is the property of the Birmingham *Evening Mail*. There's a date as well. Twenty-fourth October, 1957—not all that old is it? We can check with the papers around that period—no doubt this wedding would be reported. Mrs. Dowd is there, too—recognize her?"

Kilby shook his head, but Gwyn Thomas said, "I do. Was she famous then?"

"No. That was long after her time, but she was still well known by name, if not by sight. I'm going to enquire at the *Evening Mail* offices tomorrow. Now, back to the best man, Sergeant Kilby. Can we say that he is the man now in Leeds City mortuary."

"Can I cover his head up, sir. Make him look bald or something . . ." and Hamilton pushed a slip of paper across the photograph, just above the best man's eyes.

"There, Sergeant!"

"Mmm. I'd say it was him, sir. I think that is our man."

"Good. Then we'll have the best man identified. What about your body, Inspector Thomas? Have you spotted him?"

"No, sir. There's no one that resembles him. I see Mrs. Dowd is on the front row of that photo, sir—a parent of one of the happy couple. Do we know which?"

"No, we don't. We can find no record of her children's whereabouts. She hasn't kept an address book and the neighbours can't help. However, the press have got the story, and we've asked for their assistance in tracing them. That wedding picture could be of a son or a daughter."

Gwyn Thomas spoke. "I have a friend outside, sir, waiting in the car. I think he should see these."

"A friend?"

"A close personal friend, who is not in the force. He witnessed the fatal accident in York and saw the driver of the car in question; in fact, he drew my attention to the similarities in the two accidents. A good man, sir. I'd like him to see these photographs—the driver or his companion might be here, too. It's a chance we can't miss."

"I agree by all means—fetch him along, Inspector. Reed!" the Superintendent called a constable's name. "Organize coffee for us all will you? I don't care where you get it, so long as we don't have to pay!"

"Sir," and a tall, youthful constable left the room.

As Gwyn went for Ross MacAllister, Hamilton turned his attention to Sergeant Kilby. "Found the car that killed your man, Sergeant?"

"Not before I left, sir. The night shift had a description—scanty though it was—and there's no doubt the front of the vehicle will be damaged and bloodstained. We found some glass at the scene too, so the headlamps will be broken, I'm sure.

If it's in Leeds, our lads will turn it up before dawn."

"Inspector Thomas from York thinks theirs is stolen—he discussed it with one of my staff earlier, but I don't think he's traced it yet. Hello, here he comes."

Gwyn Thomas bounded into the room. "He's not there, sir. Must have gone to stretch his legs."

"Daft thing to do, Inspector, if I may say so."

"I've checked with the man on the door. He saw him get out of my car, sir, and walk towards the shopping centre. Half an hour ago."

"Time he was back, but we can wait. I've ordered coffee for us. Now, this casualty of yours, Inspector. He had this address in his pocket, had he not?"

"Yes, sir. On a printed card."

"That's feasible. Mrs. Dowd did take in lodgers from time to time, although I don't think she kept a regular boarding house—her register shows irregular visitors. She didn't advertise so we think she allowed persons who were mainly friends or contacts to use the place."

"I see. Well, our man had no other documents with him, except a wallet full of money. Two hundred and fifty pounds in notes to be exact, and a Yale Key No. 486772."

"Have you got it?"

"Yes, in an envelope in my file," and Gwyn Thomas produced the key.

"It might fit this house. No time like the present," and Superintendent Hamilton left the room, went downstairs and tried the key.

"There," he said, "it fits. It's the key to this house. What does that prove, Inspector?"

"Nothing that the visiting card couldn't tell us, sir."

"A little more, I think, Inspector Thomas. It shows he had permission to come to this house any time he wished—a key surely proves such permission, don't you agree? Visiting cards are handed out to any visitor as an inducement to return, but keys are rather special."

"I follow, sir."

"Which, going to a further logical conclusion, makes your man rather well known to the late Mrs. Dowd, does it not?"

"It seems like it."

"Well known enough to be a son, maybe?"

"I can't say that, can I?"

"No, we can't, but it is a thought we'll have to keep in mind, Inspector. How old is your deceased man?"

"Forty-five, I'd say. Maybe even fifty."

"And she was a shade over sixty-five, at a guess. Maybe as much as seventy. Yes, they could be mother and son. It's a line we'll have to pursue. I must contact Somerset House to find out her family history."

"You'll keep in touch with us, sir?"

"Of course, Inspector. We're all in this together. Now, while we're waiting for that coffee, tell me all about your fatal accident. Then you tell me about yours, Sergeant Kilby."

As Gwyn Thomas began his narrative, the coffee arrived; it came from a mobile police canteen just outside, and was hot and sweet. Gwyn told this huge Scotsman all the details, and in turn Sergeant Kilby outlined his story.

Hamilton nodded from time to time, grunting and supping noisily from his mug.

When both men had finished he said, "Mmm. Undoubtedly there's a strong link between the three deaths, gentlemen. And because I think along these lines, two things worry me."

"Sir?" asked Gwyn Thomas.

"Her two daughters. I'm assuming, for the sake of argument, that both dead men are her sons; it's possible, as I think you'll agree. She has two daughters as well. Where are they?"

"I see, but my man isn't on that wedding photograph, sir," put in Gwyn.

"He might have been away, or in hospital, or simply a black sheep."

"I take your point."

"Then I think we'd better trace the daughters; perhaps the bride on the photograph is one of them."

"Should we release this picture to the press?" suggested Kilby.

"I think we should, Sergeant. The National dailies." He bellowed, "Sergeant," and a uniformed sergeant clicked to attention at the doorway. "Organize a press conference at the police station for three o'clock in the morning, will you? Tell those sharks outside—they'll have missed their midnight deadline by now, anyway, and at least the TV wizards will flood the country tomorrow. Now, where's your friend, Inspector? It's time he was back."

"I'll go and have another look," said Gwyn Thomas.

He paused at the doorway and spoke to the constable on duty.

"I asked you about a friend of mine—half an hour ago," he reminded the constable.

"Yes, sir. I remember. He hasn't come back."

"The silly young buck! It's not like him to go off like this!"

Gwyn cast a glance at his car, parked a few yards away up the street, but it was still empty.

He went back indoors, puzzled.

And worried.

Ross MacAllister found himself in a back kitchen, lying on a cold tiled floor and gazing at the stained ceiling. He saw chair legs and a table above him; trousers and a pair of slender female legs in clear coloured tights.

He groaned involuntarily, and the girl said, "He's awake, Rodney."

"Help him up."

Willing hands helped Ross into a sitting position, and his eyes closed against the pain in his head; throbbing, dull pains pounding through his battered brain.

"Where am I?" he muttered.

"Who are you?" countered a voice, somewhere out of his vision.

"Ross MacAllister," he said promptly, "who are you?"

He opened his eyes and looked around; the slim faced villain was sitting on a chair at the table, sipping another drink. A girl with long blonde hair sat opposite, and there was someone else behind Ross, holding him upright.

"I'm all right." He tried to stand up, but strong hands held him down. "No, you stay right there, MacAllister," said a broad Midlands voice.

"As you say."

Ross found his head was clearing; it ached interminably at the back where he had received the blow, but he could see clearly and his mind was working quickly.

The sharp featured youth spoke, and his accent was very upper crust, "Why were you following me: Are you a police officer?"

"I wasn't following you. I was wandering about."

"I see by this that you are a salesman," and the man held up Ross's wallet.

"Yes. I work for a firm selling office

materials and I was wandering around Edgbaston. I couldn't sleep."

"You live near York."

"A village just outside York," and Ross suddenly realized the implication of this address. They must connect it somehow with the hit-and-run accident!

"What are you doing here?"

"Business," he said. "I couldn't sleep so I was wandering around."

"You followed me from Albany Crescent?"

"Where's that?" put in Ross.

They didn't reply, but clearly they thought he was a detective.

"He's not a detective!" hissed the girl. "He'd have had a notebook or a pocket radio or something."

"Detective, me? You must be joking!" He tried to sound nonchalant. "Come on, lads. Let me go. There's been enough of this tomfoolery."

"He followed me from Albany Crescent," persisted the sharp faced youth. "He waited outside the snack bar and he followed me into the gents. That's evidence enough for me!"

The man rose from his seat, and Ross saw in his hand, the slender form of a hypodermic syringe.

"What..." and he rolled over to escape. But strong hands held him down; he began to kick, but the man with the syringe fell across his legs and in a vicious, jabbing movement, the point of the syringe buried itself in Ross's thigh.

"Ah!" he screamed as the plunger was pressed home. "You bastards... what is it?"

"Something to keep you quiet for a while," they said and he found himself drifting into oblivion. He fought and fought.

But it was no good. The drug beat him and he sank into a deep, deep sleep.

"Let's get rid of him," said the sharp featured youth.

6

MEANWHILE in York, the stolen car specialists had removed the Ford Escort to the yard behind the police station, and were giving the vehicle the full treatment. It had been fingerprinted from top to bottom; this had been done twice, and then the interior of the vehicle had been stripped completely. It carried no Excise licence and the dashboard shelves had been cleared.

The seats had been removed and the bits and pieces which had slipped down were carefully examined too. Sweet papers, a sixpence, a short pencil. A button from a coat. All were taken out, examined and listed.

But the main item here was a bus ticket, for the Midland Red; it had a "V" mark clipped in the side, and was a fortnight old. The CID took it, photographed it, and rang Birmingham Police to have enquiries made about the route or other points of interest regarding this tiny slip of paper.

But the Midland area was the clue, and the CID was asked to make enquiries about the Ford Escort and they were given the chassis number and the engine number, which in this case were the same.

York asked Birmingham to search their stolen car records for a Ford Escort, dark green colour, and asked them to check further with the engine numbers, which would be in the owner's log book. The night duty clerk in Birmingham CID agreed to the request and said he'd ring back; at this stage he had no reason to connect this enquiry with the murder at Edgbaston.

For him, the job wasn't a long one. It meant checking the entire list of stolen vehicles which were maintained in numerical form, and which amounted to hundreds each month. Nationally the numbers were colossal.

He searched down the list which started at those whose numbers began with figure one; he carried on tediously, through twos and threes, sighing and grunting. There were better things to do than checking a list of vehicles. . . .

Then he found one. Stolen in Birmingham three days ago, during the night of Monday/Tuesday. A green Ford Escort, stolen from outside a house near the city centre, Reg. Number MOF 434 Z.

From the Stripdex system which gave only the barest essentials, he turned to the file of stolen vehicles, again kept in numerical order and in the section for "4" he turned up MOF 434 Z.

"That's it!" He grinned with satisfaction. "That's the one. The chassis number tallies. Recovered in York, eh?"

He put a pencil note against the number and rang York police with his information.

"Yes, it's here. The chassis number tallies. A dark green Ford stolen in Birmingham on Monday night. Yes, I can inform the owner, but you don't want him to collect it yet? Oh, it's been involved in a hit-and-run and you want time to examine it. I see. I'll keep the owner in suspense, I think—if we tell him we've found it, he'll want to go straight up to York to collect it. Anyway, thanks for telling us."

The York man thanked him for the information, then said, "Can you connect me with Inspector Thomas? He's from York; he's down there assisting with a murder enquiry."

"We can't telephone him, but I can get a message to the scene by radio."

"Good. Tell him about the Ford, will you? It's connected with that killing at Edgbaston."

"Is it, by jove! OK. I'll pass the details on. Cheerio."

Inspector Thomas received the news with happiness and passed it quickly to Superintendent Hamilton.

"So the car was stolen here, eh? Nasty. This brings us back to Birmingham again.

Now, Sergeant Kilby—I wonder how your force is getting along with your killer car? I'd like to bet it was stolen here too!"

"I'll give them a ring, sir, and find out. They might have found it abandoned."

"Do that. You can't ring from here, we haven't got an extension yet, so get one of the cars to run you down to the office."

"Thank you, sir," and Sergeant Kilby left the room.

Hamilton turned to Gwyn Thomas. "No sign of your friend, Inspector."

"No, sir. I'm worried now. I'm wondering if he's got involved in something connected with this killing."

"How? By just sitting in a car?"

"You don't know Ross MacAllister, sir! I've never come across a more trouble-prone character in all my life. He's a wizard at getting involved in things—this affair is a good example."

"Think he's seen something?"

"What else? He wouldn't wander off without letting us know, and I know he wanted to come in here. I said he couldn't without your permission; I wish I had now."

"He's not a policeman then?"

"Oh, no. A civilian—a salesman in fact. I'll nip out and ask if any of the pressmen saw him wandering off. They've got eyes like hawks."

"Do that."

Once more, Gwyn Thomas found himself at the front door of number forty-two Albany Crescent and before he spoke, the duty constable said, "He's not back yet, sir."

"Thanks. I'll have words with the press. They might have seen something."

He walked towards the little knot of pressmen who were waiting hopefully outside and, as he approached, flash bulbs began to burst into life and cameras clicked.

As one, the chorus of pressmen demanded news; they pressed him for a statement.

"Nothing doing, lads. You'll have to ask Superintendent Hamilton about that. My problem is more immediate. I've lost a friend of mine—he was sitting in my car over there," and he pointed to his car. "He got out and he's vanished. I wondered if you hawk-eyed chaps had seen him?"

"What's he look like?" asked one of the reporters.

"Thirty or thereabouts. Tall chap, very athletic; dark hair and sports clothes."

"I saw him!" cried a small man at the back. "But that was a long time ago—almost an hour, I'd say."

"What happened?" pressed Gwyn.

"He got out and came this way, past us. He was following another man."

"Following another man?" cried Gwyn. "And you didn't follow him? You call yourselves pressmen?" he added good humouredly.

"Why? What's going on?"

"Look," he held up his hand, "I don't know. Can you describe the man he followed?"

Someone else piped up, "It was that funny bloke standing next to me. Bit queer if you ask me."

"What did he look like?" persisted Gwyn.

"Young chap with long hair."

"What sort of face?"

"Staring eyes. Long pointed features, sir."

"And his clothes?"

"One of those suède jackets—a dark one. Dark brown, I think, but it wasn't easy to see in this light. He was standing right next to me."

"Thanks," and Gwyn turned to walk away. But the press surrounded him.

"Why? Who was he? Who's your friend? Is he a policeman? A detective? Was it the killer?"

They threw the questions at him in rapid succession, but he forced himself away from them; Ross MacAllister had done it again!

In the whole of Birmingham, he had found the very man who was in the killer car in York and had followed him. Of that fact, there was no doubt in Gwyn Thomas's mind. But where had they gone?

Why hadn't Ross telephoned in?

Damn the man! For a moment, Gwyn Thomas wasn't thinking of the case—he was thinking of Maureen MacAllister and her family.

Ross MacAllister returned to consciousness to find himself in a single bed which was tucked into the corner of a tiny bedroom. The curtains were closed and there was a low light in the room.

For a moment he lay in the bed, looking at the ceiling. Plain white, and very clean; the paper on the walls was clean and he saw coloured pictures of pop groups and film stars pasted across the walls. A teenager's room.

Then he tried to sit up; he felt dizzy and collapsed on to the pillow again, panting and perspiring slightly. He turned his head; there was a girl sitting in a basketwork chair not far from the bedside. She was watching him, her long blonde hair cascading across her shoulders.

"Hello," she said.

"Hello," he grunted, turning to face her. "Who are you?" It was the girl he'd seen before, just after he'd been clubbed.
"My name is Kathy."
"Can I get up?"
"You haven't any clothes on."
He looked down in horror; he was covered in blankets and he saw the grin on her face.
"Where are they?"
"They're safe."
"Where am I?"
"Somewhere in the Birmingham area, Mr. MacAllister."
He propped himself up on his elbow, wondering how she would stop him from leaving the room; his head buzzed and ached. The room swam, and he didn't say anything.
"Shy?"
"Who me?" he managed to say. "I'm married, Kathy. I don't mind parading in front of you—you'd be the embarrassed one, not me. Now, I'm in a house, so there must be some clothes somewhere."
He eased himself a little further into a

sitting position. "And if I decide to look for them, you'll have a job to stop me."

"I don't think so," she smiled, and he saw a small automatic pistol in her hands; it had been hidden behind the handbag on her knee. "I have used this before, Mr. MacAllister, and if you try to get out of that bed, for any reason at all, I shall use it again."

"Mmm." He sank back into the pillows. "What time is it?"

"Nearly three o'clock."

"Are we still in Thursday night? Well, Friday morning?"

"We are—Friday morning."

"What's happening next?"

"My friends will be coming to take you away, Mr. MacAllister."

"Where to?"

"How should I know? They don't tell me everything. They think you are a policeman."

"Rubbish! I'm a salesman. What are they going to do with me?"

She shrugged her shoulders. "I don't know."

He looked across at her; a pretty girl with long blonde hair; she was dressed in a pale blue sweater and a dark blue mini skirt which showed off her thighs. Firm breasted and slender; she'd be about twenty or twenty-two. No more.

"Who are your friends?" he began to question the girl.

"I'm not saying."

"Maybe you don't know them?"

"Of course I know them!" Her eyes flashed. "You are being silly and I won't fall for any of your questioning. You are going to stay in that bed until my friends come. They'll be here shortly."

He sank into the pillow, lying with his hands behind his head trying to think.

They didn't know him. They didn't know what part he was playing in the enquiry, and obviously they felt he knew more than he did. They were going to get rid of him, it seemed. Get him out of the way....

Who was the girl? Kathy? He recalled Sergeant Kilby's account of the Leeds fatal accident, when a witness said there was a woman in the killer car. This girl?

"Were you in Leeds today?" he asked her suddenly.

She smiled. "Find out," was her only reply, and her lips closed in a tight, firm line.

"York then?"

"Find that out too!"

"You know about the accidents?" Ross persisted.

"Accidents?" Her pretty brow creased into a puzzled frown.

"The murders, then. In York and Leeds this afternoon."

"I don't know what you are talking about." And again her pretty face showed signs of uncertainty, bewilderment.

"Two killings. Hit-and-run accidents, both using stolen cars. Two men in the York car, and a man and a woman in the Leeds one. Deliberate killings at twelve-thirty this afternoon, and the woman in the Leeds car was a blonde. Like you!"

"Then it wasn't me!"

"Wasn't it?" Ross hauled himself on to

his elbow, resting his head on his hand. He faced her. "We have a witness who saw you, Kathy. Saw you in the passenger seat of a car which deliberately ran down and killed a pedestrian in Leeds."

"No, it's not true! You are a policeman!"

"And our witness is a first class one; we have an Identikit picture of the girl in that car, and she looks just like you. So you're going to find yourself on a murder charge, Kathy!"

"No! You can't. It wasn't me...." She changed the subject rapidly. "You seem to know a lot about the accidents."

"We know they are connected with the murder of Mrs. Dowd. We know an awful lot about these killings, Kathy. And so do you!"

"Oh, God!"

And the door opened. In burst the slender youth with long hair, who said, "He sounds wide awake, Kathy."

She sighed with relief, left the chair and ran to him.

"Slim! He knows. He's a copper, I'm sure . . ."

"Knows? Knows what?"

"About York and Leeds. . . ."

"What's he know about York and Leeds?" There was a savage tone in his voice, and the youth, known as Slim, sat down on the bed, facing Ross. "Come on, MacAllister. What have you been telling Kathy? Frightening her?"

"Nothing. I merely said we know all about the connection between the accidents in York and Leeds and the murder of Mrs. Dowd."

His face paled. "God! Of course . . . you're from York! Kathy—get Rodney!"

She hurried from the room, as Slim paced up and down, chin in his hands, clearly nervous. A highly strung youth; the youth he'd seen clutching the dashboard of that Ford Escort.

"Then you are the police? God . . . this is awful."

Slim had his back to Ross; he had stopped in his tracks, head bowed in thought. They hadn't realized the connection between Ross and York . . . they hadn't suspected for a moment that the police knew that there was any connection between the three killings. . . .

Then Ross moved.

Like lightning he flung back the bedclothes and leapt from the bed; he was wearing underpants, he found. He leapt for the back of the skinny youth, who turned at the sounds behind him.

But Ross had him. As Slim half-turned, Ross's right hand came down across his throat with all the strength he could muster. Slim sank to the floor, gurgling and unconscious as Ross bent down to listen to his breathing. He was all right. He'd be unconscious for twenty minutes or so.

Frantically, Ross began to strip off the clothes of this man; first the sweater, then the pants.

Then sounds outside. Heavy footsteps. This must be Rodney or the girl returning.

Ross stepped behind the door to wait.

7

A MAN appeared, slowly at first, then, seeing his fallen companion, rushed into the room to attend to him. Ross crashed his clasped fists on the back of the man's neck. He fell like a log across his friend, and moaned softly. Then he, too, was still. It was the man called Rodney.

Quickly Ross shut the door. There was no one else. He pulled off Rodney's jacket.

Urgently he dressed himself in the tight trousers and sweater from the fallen Slim, then Rodney's jacket. A pair of soft and pliable shoes from Slim, tight, but not too uncomfortable. It was time to leave.

Outside the room, he came upon a large landing, dull and ill lit, with four or five doors leading from it; a flight of carpeted stairs. He ran down the stairs; another flight lay ahead of him.

Down those too, running quickly. Lights in some of the rooms. A radio softly playing foreign music. Otherwise, silence.

Ross was at the foot of the stairs; there was a commotion above. Men shouting. Noise.

"Stop that man!" yelled a man's voice. "For God's sake stop him!"

The door was ahead; the borrowed shoes were beginning to hurt as Ross made his dash for freedom. The door was held on a Yale lock; he slipped it open and in a moment was outside. Outside in the gloom and darkness of an unknown street. There was a number twelve on the door.

But where was he?

Which way? Left or right?

He chose the right, towards lights at the end of the street. He sought some indication of his present whereabouts. A street name. A shop. A pub. Anything.

Then the door thrown open behind him cast a patch of clear light across the street.

Voices sounding harsh in the darkness. Panic and anger.

"There he is!"

Footsteps behind him. Ross ran, seeking shelter, shadows, side turnings, anywhere to fade away. They would know this part of Birmingham like the backs of their hands. He didn't know it at all.

He was almost at the end of the street; it spread into a broad junction with another thoroughfare, well lit by sodium lighting; there was a traffic island in the middle; a bus shelter and a taxi rank with waiting taxis.

"Taxi!" He found himself panting heavily.

He ran across the road, heedless of the night traffic. A taxi crept forward towards him. The driver must have sensed the urgency for he had opened a rear door and Ross leapt inside.

"Thank God!" he said. "Take me to forty-two Albany Crescent, quick!"

"Albany Crescent?"

"Yes. In Edgbaston."

"Oh, I know it."

"What's this place?" asked Ross.

"The Bull Ring. You in trouble?"

"Nearly was," and he turned to see the two men emerge into the glare of the street lighting. They stopped as the taxi drove away, carrying their prey.

"What's that street?" asked Ross.

"Which?"

"The one I just ran out of."

"Fern Street."

"Thanks. Now, fast as you can to Albany Crescent—it's police business."

"You'll be there in a jiff, mate."

As the taxi drew up outside Mrs. Dowd's house, Ross put his hand into his pocket to pay; then he realized he wasn't wearing his own clothes and he had no money.

"Damn!" he cursed.

"Twenty-two shillings, mate," said the taxi-driver, holding out his hand.

"These aren't my clothes," Ross tried to explain. "They've taken mine. Hang on—I'll call that young PC on the door," and with that, he whistled loudly.

The policeman called out, "I can't leave this door, sir."

"Shout for Inspector Thomas, will you? Tell him Ross MacAllister's here, and needs help."

"Right, sir."

"This the murder place, mate?" asked the cabby.

"That's the spot," Ross told him. "Things are getting exciting—thanks for getting me here like you did—sorry to keep you waiting for the cash. Ah! He's coming now."

The tall figure of Gwyn Thomas, with a pipe in his mouth, was trotting down the steps towards the taxi.

As he neared it, he removed the pipe and bent down to the window. Ross spoke, "It's me Gwyn, I'm in a bit of bother."

"And where the hell have you been, Ross? I've been worried sick. . . ."

"Look, it's a long story, but this gentleman wants paying and I've no money."

"No money!"

"I've had to change my clothes.... Look, Gwyn, pay up, man, and I'll explain inside."

"How much?"

"I'll take a quid," agreed the cabby, and Gwyn Thomas stuffed a note in his hand, plus a half-crown tip.

Ross climbed out, looking untidy and dishevelled, and the taxi drove away.

Gwyn said, "Now, Ross. What's been going on?"

Once they were inside the building, Ross rapidly explained the situation to Gwyn Thomas and Superintendent Hamilton.

"Send a car round to number twelve Fern Street—Quickly!" ordered Hamilton as the story unfolded. "Surround the place. We'll all go and break in!"

"Are you sure Slim was the passenger in the car at York?" asked Gwyn Thomas.

"No doubt at all. And the girl—I tackled her about being in the Leeds car, but she wouldn't admit it. In fact, she seemed puzzled by mention of the accidents."

"Get any names from them?" asked Hamilton.

"The sharp featured lad is called Slim and the girl is Kathy. The other one—a heavy built youth, is called Rodney. I'm sure he was driving the car at York!"

"Then this is the lead we need. My men are on their way to Fern Street; I'd like you to have a look through our Rogues Gallery, Mr. MacAllister. See if you can identify your men."

"My pleasure."

"Right. I want to go to number twelve Fern Street."

Then Hamilton bellowed "Sergeant" to no one in particular, and a uniformed sergeant appeared. "Sergeant, take Mr. MacAllister to Headquarters, will you? I want him to look through our photographs. Fix it up, will you? What about you, Inspector Thomas?"

"I'd like to go with Ross, sir? I think someone had better keep an eye on him."

"As you wish. I think you've done all

you can here. What about Sergeant Kilby?"

"I think he's finished, hasn't he? Look, sir. I can follow the sergeant in my car, then we can go straight home afterwards. It'll save time."

"All right. Go and find Kilby and we'll get going. I'm going to Fern Street."

"I'll leave a note of any positive identifications in your Headquarters, sir."

"Do that, Inspector. Thanks for calling. Must dash off now," and he left them.

Sergeant Kilby appeared and joined Ross and Gwyn Thomas. They followed the Birmingham City Police car to its Headquarters, and were taken into a well lighted room somewhere on the third floor of the building.

As they went into the room, Gwyn Thomas laughed. "I wish you could see yourself now, Ross! You look a proper clip! Dead fashionable, those clothes!"

"It's not funny, Gwyn! This is the second time I've been stripped of my clothes on this case! I think I'll sue for a replacement outfit!"

"You'd never succeed, my dear friend. Anyway, let's get this job done, then we can go home. What time is it now?"

"Gone half-past three!"

"Mmm. It's going to be late by the time we get home. Ah, here are the photographs now."

The sergeant put half a dozen bound albums in front of them, and said, "Top one is the most recent, sir. I'd start there."

"Are they all local convicts?"

"Convicted persons, suspected persons and those likely to commit crime."

"Good. Well, Ross. Off you go. See if your friends at number twelve Fern Street are here."

Superintendent Hamilton had two car loads of men at number twelve Fern Street and he joined them within minutes of their arrival. One car load was at the rear, while the other supervised the front door.

"Right. One man on the front door; one in the car. The rest of us inside." He addressed the men in the main street, "I've had words with the lads out at the back. They're doing the same."

A constable and a sergeant, both in uniform, came forward and volunteered to go in with Hamilton.

"Right. MacAllister mentioned coming down two flights of stairs, so we're interested in the second floor."

"These houses are let off in flats, sir," the sergeant told him. "One flat per storey."

"Thanks. That's useful to know. Ready."

Both men nodded, and Hamilton led them in. The entrance hall was comparatively well lit, and after making sure there was a constable in position at the door, Hamilton led his men upstairs.

He made no attempt to enter any room on the first floor, as, with his assistants in close attendance, he climbed higher, motioning for silence. On the second landing Hamilton stopped. "Sergeant.

Stay here—watch every door. Constable —you come in with me. Right?"

"Sir," acknowledged the two men.

Hamilton went to the door on his immediate left; in his hand he held a long handled torch. He opened the door into a void of blackness and flashed his light around the room. Then he switched on the light.

"Nothing!"

Similarly with the other rooms. Empty.

"All empty," said Hamilton with no surprise in his voice. "The birds have flown. It was obvious they would."

"What about the other flats, sir?"

"Might have holed up there—with friends. OK. Let's do the whole building while we're here."

The couple in the flat beneath objected most strongly to the police intrusion.

"No! Have you a warrant?"

"No, I haven't," snapped Hamilton. "But two murderers were in the flat above less than half an hour ago. They might be here."

"Let him in," said the woman, a frail,

pale faced woman in her mid-thirties. "It's for our own good."

"But they have no warrant . . ."

"Then you search for them!" snapped Hamilton. "You search for the two killers."

"No, no. Come along in. But I'm going to protest to my MP for your intrusion . . . my wife and I."

"Be quiet, John," pleaded the woman. "You're never at your best when you've just woken."

The man called John flopped into an arm-chair and grunted to himself. He pulled a dressing gown tight around himself, as his wife, pretty in a fragile sort of way, gave every assistance to Superintendent Hamilton.

Then, satisfied that no one else was in the flat, Hamilton said, "Do you know the people above?"

"No. I thought there was only one man above us. I saw those youngsters last night for the first time. I don't know them at all."

The husband spoke now, "The

previous tenant was a nice chap. A Mr. Hewitt. A very nice man."

"And has he left?"

"We didn't think so, but we didn't see him around yesterday and then yesterday evening, those youngsters arrived."

"Is the flat furnished?"

"Oh, yes. They're all furnished."

"And the landlord?"

"She lives two doors away at number ten. A Miss Birtle—she lives in the ground floor flat of that house."

"Thanks. Look, I might want another word with you? Can you wait up for half an hour? It is important."

The man looked across at his wife, and was about to say something about needing his sleep, when she smiled and said, "Of course. I'll put the kettle on."

The people in the ground floor flat were more co-operative, and a thorough search revealed no one answering the descriptions supplied by Ross MacAllister. Nor could they say much about the people upstairs—except that a quiet man, Mr. Hewitt, lived in the top flat.

Hamilton thanked them; the next job was to get Mr. Hewitt identified.

He returned to the young couple, and found a cup of tea waiting.

"Most kind of you, Mrs. . . ."

"Silsford," she said. "Susan Silsford. My husband, John."

"Hamilton is my name," boomed the Superintendent. "Must say you're most co-operative, especially after being roused in the middle of the night. Now, what can you tell me about Mr. Hewitt?"

They sipped the tea and discussed their problem.

"Not a great deal. I don't even know where he works, but he looks like a businessman or an office worker."

"Age? Height? Accent?"

"Oh, hard to say. Quite tall."

"Taller than me?" put in Hamilton.

"No. Just under six feet," said John Silsford. "About forty—maybe even forty-two or three. Dark hair, going slightly bald. Average sort of build, I'd say."

"He has no real accent, has he, John?"

put in his wife. "It's like those men on the BBC television. Nothing definite."

"Yes, that's true."

"Is he always smartly dressed?"

"Always. Dark suits, as a rule."

"Does he have many visitors? Did those youngsters come before?"

"I never saw them before," said Susan Silsford, "and I'm around most of the day . . . I don't work, you see. I'm . . ."

"We're expecting a child in a few months," put in John Silsford by way of explanation. "But Mr. Hewitt lives a very quiet life. I can't remember anyone calling on him."

"Has he been here long?"

"He was here when we came, Superintendent," John Silsford told him. "But we've only been here for five months."

"When did you last see him?"

"Let me see . . . it's Thursday now . . ." began Susan Silsford.

"Friday," corrected her husband, "Friday morning. Four o'clock! I saw him on Tuesday. He left here about quarter-to-nine on Tuesday morning."

"On his way to work?"

"He usually left at that time, but he had a small suitcase with him on Tuesday. A week-end case."

"Does he sometimes go away on business?"

"Not very often. Once a month, maybe. At least, I've seen him with a suitcase about once a month."

"Any idea where he goes?"

Both John Silsford and his wife shook their heads. "Sorry."

"Good. Well thanks for your help. I'll have to knock your landlady out of bed now. Miss Birtle, you say she's called."

"Yes."

"Well thanks for your help, Mr. and Mrs. Silsford. I might want to speak to you again, but it will keep until morning. Thanks again for your co-operation."

"Good-bye."

Outside, the sergeant said, "Think they're all right, sir?"

Hamilton pursed his lips. "Yes. Honest as the day they were born. They're not hiding anything. Right. I want the constables to remain on the doors until they get relieved. They must check anyone who comes in or out. Our Mr. Hewitt looks as though he has some explaining to do."

Miss Birtle was a lady nearing sixty, who lived in a miserable little furnished flat at number ten but she was affable enough.

"I heard the commotion, Superintendent," she told him. "It woke me up, you know."

"Did you look out?"

"Yes. Two men and a girl left the flats shortly before you came. They were running towards the Bull Ring."

"Damn!" spat Hamilton. "Who were they?"

"I don't know, Superintendent. It was too dark to see them, but I haven't anyone of that description in my flats."

"Mr. Hewitt lives in the top flat of number twelve, doesn't he?"

"Oh, yes. A very good tenant, Superintendent."

"Has he terminated his tenancy?"

"Oh no."

"But we have reason to think those youngsters were in his flat."

"Then unless they were his guests, they had no right, Superintendent. Mr. Hewitt is a nice man, you know. He doesn't encourage that sort of person."

"Where does he work?"

"I can't tell you, I'm afraid. I think he works in the city. A businessman, I think—he goes off sometimes. I guessed they were business trips."

"I believe he left on Tuesday."

"Yes. He told me on Monday evening when I saw him."

"Did he say where he was going, Miss Birtle?"

"Yes. He said he was going to Leeds."

"Leeds!" exploded Hamilton. "Leeds! Sergeant—get on to the car radio and ring Headquarters. Catch Sergeant Kilby before he sets off back to Leeds. He's got a photograph of the victim in that road accident—I want Miss Birtle to see it."

8

MEANWHILE, in Birmingham City Police Headquarters, Ross MacAllister pointed excitedly to a photograph.

"This one, Sergeant. Number eight on page fourteen. That is the driver of the car, I'm sure..."

"How positive are you, Mr. Mac-Allister?"

"As positive as I can be," and Ross turned to Gwyn Thomas seated beside him, "I'd swear that's the driver, Gwyn —the man called Rodney."

"Good. Can we have him identified, Sergeant?"

"Yes, sir."

The duty sergeant brought across an index and flicked it open to the corresponding page.

"Here we are—you're right. It is Rodney Hill, born 15.3.1943, at Selly

Oak, Birmingham. Five foot nine inches tall, heavy build, dark brown hair, inclined to be curly. Home address: 213 Conway Road, Conway Estate, Birmingham."

"What's he been in for?"

"Two convictions—both for possessing dangerous drugs, heroin mainly."

"A drug pusher!" breathed Gwyn Thomas. "Hey, this might be what we're looking for, Ross. Drugs!"

"I'll send a car round to his address, sir."

"Yes, do that, Sergeant. If he's at home, bring him here on suspicion of murder."

"Sir," and the duty sergeant went off to arrange for a crime car to visit Conway Estate.

"Ross. What about your pal with the sharp features. Slim. See if he's here, will you?"

As Ross searched the albums, Sergeant Kilby and Gwyn Thomas looked for pictures of the two deceased persons, but each drew a blank. It seemed the victims were Birmingham people. But there was no photograph of the youth with sharp features and Ross sighed, "Well, at least we've done something useful, Gwyn. Do we need to stay any longer?"

"I don't think so. The City has got everything well under control now. I suppose we are superfluous to their requirements. Even if they do arrest Hill, they have first chance to indict him for murder, or at the very least, conspiracy to murder! There's enough circumstantial evidence to involve Hill, I'd say."

The telephone rang.

The duty sergeant was still organizing enquiries from Conway Estate, so Gwyn Thomas answered it.

"Detective Inspector Thomas."

"Information Room here, sir. Have you a Sergeant Kilby with you, from Leeds City."

"Yes, he's here. Who wants him?"

"I've got a wireless call from Superintendent Hamilton. He wants to know if Sergeant Kilby's still there, and secondly, if he'll take his file on the Leeds accident round to number ten Fern Street. It's the photograph he wants."

"Right. We'll come. Where's Fern Street?"

"Just off the Bull Ring. Can't miss it. Look for the Gas Showrooms on the corner and turn off there."

"We're on our way."

They arrived to see Hamilton's car parked outside number ten, but Ross said, "It's the wrong house, Gwyn. I was in number twelve."

"He said ten in the message, Ross."

"We'll have to try ten, Gwyn—his car's there."

They parked behind Hamilton's car and walked towards number ten Fern Street; as they approached, the door opened and Hamilton blocked it with his immense figure.

"Come along in. Glad you didn't get away, chaps."

He led them into the cosy room which Miss Birtle used as her lounge, and there was an electric fire burning in the grate. Miss Birtle had donned a warm dressing gown and was beaming all over with the excitement of a police visit.

Hamilton introduced everyone.

"This is Miss Birtle," he said, "she is the landlady of the flat at number twelve —where you, Mr. MacAllister, were held prisoner. Now the youngsters you saw there seem to have had no right in that flat. The top flat is rented to a Mr. Hewitt, and he has not terminated his tenancy. He was last seen on Tuesday, before going to Leeds on a business trip."

"Leeds?" queried Gwyn Thomas.

"Rings a bell, doesn't it. So it is at this point I want Sergeant Kilby to show his photographs to Miss Birtle. All right, Sergeant? Be discreet."

Obviously, Miss Birtle had no idea what was in store for her and Hamilton was saying, "This won't be very pleasant, Miss Birtle, but Sergeant Kilby will spare you the worst. Carry on, Sergeant."

Kilby had a head and shoulders shot of the man in Leeds Mortuary, and decided to use this one. He covered the part which showed the badly torn neck with his hands, and then brought it forward to show the elderly lady.

"Take your time," advised Kilby. "Take a good look at him."

She sat on the edge of her chair, fingers in her mouth, and it was evident that she was nervous. But Kilby's gentleness won the day; the picture was beneath her face now and she was looking down at the calm features of the dead man.

She began to nod slowly, and the triumph of Hamilton's face was wonderful to see.

"It's him, Superintendent. That's my Mr. Hewitt . . . oh, dear . . ." and she began to weep.

"We'll need formal evidence of identification for the inquest, sir," reminded Sergeant Kilby.

"I think we might find someone else for that task, Sergeant," said Hamilton pointedly, then he turned to Miss Birtle, "thank you for helping us, Miss Birtle. It was most kind of you. Now, can you tell us anything about Mr. Hewitt—his friends, relations, previous address?"

"No, I'm afraid not. I don't know where he came from, or anything about him. I collected his rent each Friday and we had a few words, but I never really knew him."

"Did anyone else know him?"

She shook her grey head. "I don't know. I just don't know."

"Just one more thing—his Christian name?"

"It will be in my book," and she went across to a tidy bureau in the corner of the room. From it she produced a foolscap lined book; a list of her tenants.

"Eric," she said eventually, "Eric Hewitt. He came here on the thirteenth of January—a Monday."

"No more information?"

She passed the book across to Hamilton who shook his head. "Pity. But you've been most helpful, Miss Birtle. Most helpful. Now, we'd better get back to the office, gentlemen."

"Good-bye, Superintendent."

"Good-bye, Miss Birtle—and thanks again."

They left the house and Hamilton said, "Wonderful, wonderful! We've got the Leeds man identified. So he wasn't a son either. That means we can dismiss the family motive, I think."

"Sir," said Gwyn Thomas. "There's something else we ought to tell you. Ross identified a man in your Rogues Gallery —the driver of the York car. He's one of your local drug pushers."

"A drug pusher? Who?"

There was a fierce glow in Hamilton's eyes; a glow of deep hatred.

"I hate drugs!" he spat. "I hate everything they stand for; I hate all that they do to a young body and a young mind! Who is it?"

"Rodney Hill. He lives . . ."

"I know where he lives, thank you," grunted Hamilton. "Someone gone up there?"

"Yes, sir," Gwyn told him. "A car has gone with instructions to bring him in."

"Was he in that flat, MacAllister?"

"Yes, with the blonde, Kathy, and Slim."

"They'll be far enough away by now. Now who could the blonde be? Our drug squad might help with that problem. Right, fellers. What now? I'm going back to Albany Crescent. You're welcome to come along to see what's developed, and I want to put out an All Stations call for the arrest of Rodney Hill and his companions."

"Well?" Gwyn Thomas looked at the others.

"I'm all for Albany Crescent," said Ross.

"Me too," enthused Sergeant Kilby, who had found himself involved in a case which had exceeded all his wildest dreams. "I'd better ring my office or there'll be Hell on. I didn't tell them I was coming down here!"

"Radio our Information Room from Albany Crescent," suggested Hamilton. "Come along. Follow me."

"Just a moment, sir," Ross halted. "I was taken into the back of a house, and I'm sure it was nowhere near the Bull Ring like this one. It was a similar place

"... but it wasn't far from Albany Crescent. I'm sure this is a different house."

"Would you know where to find it?"

"Yes. The door had no number, but I scribbled my initials in ball-point on the door jamb."

"Give me a rough idea—it might be en route back to Albany Crescent."

Ross explained the route he'd taken while following Slim and Hamilton nodded and grunted, working it out in his own mind.

"I know it, lad. Right—we'll pay a surprise visit on our way back."

"Do you still want a guard on number twelve, sir?"

"Oh, yes. Until dawn, or even later. One car can return to base though."

"I'd welcome the chance to get my clothes back," said Ross. "They'll be in number twelve."

"Go and look while I'm telling the men their jobs," suggested Hamilton.

He gave the orders to the waiting men and then climbed back into his own car.

Ross appeared again, happy in his own clothes which he'd found in a cupboard and Hamilton said, "Ross, you jump in beside me—we'll look for that other house."

He drove like the wind through the Birmingham streets and eventually Ross found himself on familiar ground. He recognized the snack bar, the toilets visited by Slim and then Hamilton was turning up a dark street.

"Don't tell me," Hamilton said. "Don't tell me which house. See if I can guess!"

Ross MacAllister grinned. The old fox knew! He knew which house.

The police car drew silently to a halt, and from the cubby hole, Hamilton produced a torch and shone it on the door jamb.

"There," he said proudly. "Your initials?"

"How did you know?" asked Ross.

"Rodney Hill. He used this place to push his drugs—long, long ago. The house belongs to his family—Rodney was living here for a time because his parents threw him out. They didn't like his activities."

"Does he still live here?"

"Occasionally. Let's go in, shall we, although there'll be no one here. Not now. They've had too much of a fright for one night."

Hamilton was right. The house was deserted, although the back door was ajar, and there were signs of fairly recent activity—cups of tea, fairly fresh. The warmth of a gas fire. A newspaper dated yesterday.

Hamilton gave the house a thorough search and said, "I know this place like the back of my hand. Cunning devil, is young Hill. He knows we're on to him, but he's too cute to let us catch him."

"Where's he get his supplies, sir?" asked Gwyn Thomas who had followed them in.

"Liverpool, mainly. And London. He gets them by road, I'm sure. At one time, he and his mates used the railway. They carried drugs on the trains, or hid them behind toilet cisterns, or in suitcases which they left in a special position in the corridors. But we got the British Transport police on to them, and they gave all the Birmingham to London trains a thorough going-over, day after day. So we managed to put a stop to their activities, but they've taken to the roads now."

"Private cars?"

"Almost certainly. We've come across some of his hiding places, thanks to anonymous tips from addicts he's upset by overcharging. But he's still at it, Inspector."

They were back in the kitchen of the house now.

"He'll still be in town, I've no doubt about that. I think a full press campaign is one answer now. You know the sort of thing: 'The police think Rodney Hill can assist them in their enquiries' line of attack."

"Flush him out, eh?"

"That's the general idea."

"Has he a car of his own?" asked Gwyn Thomas.

"No, that would make it too easy for our men to keep tabs on him. He borrows, hires or steals cars."

As they walked back to their parked vehicles, Ross thought hard. Drugs. Was this the line they ought to continue?

Yet why kill an old lady?

An actress. . . .

Show business?

Then like a flash out of the blue, he remembered Slim in the gents—he'd gone into a cubicle, and had come out. An ordinary set of circumstances. But the chain hadn't been pulled. Ross remembered now. No flushing . . . not particularly odd perhaps, but toilets were a favourite place for the collection or even the administering of drugs. They were left behind the cisterns of certain public toilets for collection by the addicts or the pushers.

"Sir," he addressed Superintendent Hamilton, "I think we ought to do some more investigation on the lines that drugs are the motive for the killings," and he went on to explain about the few moments in the nearby gents.

"You're right, MacAllister! That toilet has been used for pushing, and I've no doubt that long haired Slim is either hooked, or a pusher himself. Therefore, I think we ought to find out more about the unfortunate Mrs. Hannah Dowd, alias the ex-actress, Annette Wallace."

"That shouldn't be too difficult, should it?" said Gwyn. "Any daily paper will give you her life history. They're bound to have a file about her, and no doubt her obituary was written long ago."

"I'll ring the Birmingham *Evening Mail*—in fact, I'll call round now. They work all night."

"I think we'll get away back to Yorkshire, sir," suggested Gwyn Thomas.

"Nonsense. You're being wonderful down here. Come along to the newspaper offices. You'll enjoy the experience. Wonderful how these things come off the presses ready for first thing in the morning."

"I ought to ring Leeds, sir," said

Sergeant Kilby, "I want to tell them the name of our man in the morgue, and explain where I am."

"They know where you are, Sergeant. I fixed that, but you must tell them the name of your man. I suggest your night staff visit every boarding house and hotel in Leeds to see if Eric Hewitt has signed their registers."

"I'll do that, sir."

"Good. There should be a telephone link at Albany Crescent by this time. We've nattered the GPO to fix an emergency line for us. Ring from there, Sergeant. I'll be spending a few minutes in the house to assess the current situation."

Hamilton was true to his word.

He spent only the shortest time in the house and seemed quite willing to let his subordinates get along without his interference in the routine work of the investigation. His men had thoroughly fingerprinted the house from top to bottom and a forensic scientist had vacuum cleaned the murder area in the hope of picking up some minute clue.

The house had been photographed from top to bottom; the body had been examined in situ, and had now been removed to the mortuary. There would be a post mortem examination in the morning, and the removal of the body, only half an hour ago, heralded the termination of the scientific side of the investigation. All that remained was the routine; boring and tedious police work. The endless questions, the taking of countless statements. The interviews, the following of false trails. All this, and all the other odds and ends that made a murder enquiry such an immense undertaking.

And Hamilton knew that all this was being done. He had a good team, and respected them.

Before leaving, though, he mentioned that drugs—either "hard" or "soft" might be involved in the murder. A new line—a clue which might unlock the mystery of the motive for the killing. To date, there was no known motive, nor had the weapon been found.

Detective Chief Inspector Crispin, immediately in charge inside the house, ordered the Drugs Squad to be called in to undertake a thorough and specialized search of the house and premises.

But the preliminary search had not revealed anything of further interest. Mrs. Dowd's papers were dull and uninformative—she kept a few books of cuttings of her past glories, and these were included in the dossier of her murder.

But no concrete clue was discovered. Hamilton told his men to continue and told the Detective Chief Inspector where he could find him.

"The *Evening Mail*'s offices, sir?"

"Yes, Chief Inspector. I'm hoping to learn a lot more about Annette Wallace alias Hannah Dowd, deceased."

9

SERGEANT KILBY returned after calling Leeds and he had a smile on his face.

"Leeds are going to go to town on the boarding houses and hotels, sir—but other news too. A night duty PC has found the car that killed Eric Hewitt. At least, we assume it did—it has all the hallmarks of a hit-and-run car. Dent in the front nearside wing, bent bumper bar, smashed headlights. We'll be able to check against his blood group, and with particles of glass in his clothing, to establish that contact did take place."

"Stolen car, Sergeant?" asked Gwyn Thomas.

"Yes. With false plates, like yours in York. It's a light grey Triumph 2000—fairly new, but the Excise disc was still in the windscreen. It's a Birmingham car, sir, and a check with your Headquarters showed that it was stolen yesterday by garage-breaking."

"Have they fingerprinted it and so on?"

"Yes, not a trace. A clean car, I'm afraid."

"So you'll have a job to connect any of our suspects with your fatal accident?"

"I agree. A hell of a job, unless one of them cracks when we get them in. There was a girl in the car, you know—a blonde."

"I hadn't forgotten the significance of that, Sergeant Kilby. Any more phoning to do before we descend upon the Birmingham *Evening Mail?*"

They shook their heads, and he said, "Right. We'll all go in my car."

The *Evening Mail* office lay in Colmore Circus, Birmingham 4, which was also the offices of the *Birmingham Post*.

Hamilton marched into the building, past the commissionaire who recognized him, and made his way upstairs to the night editor's office.

He tapped on the door; and a man in

shirt sleeves and a harassed expression answered and said, "Yeh?"

"Detective Superintendent Hamilton," announced the brusque detective. "I'd like words with your Night Editor."

"You in charge of the Dowd murder enquiry, sir?"

"I am."

"Come in. I'll get him."

Hamilton and his colleagues entered the busy, noisy office and eventually a man signalled for them to come across to a partitioned office at the far end. They wound their way between busy desks and scurrying people.

"It never stops, does it?" muttered Hamilton.

"I expect our presence in Albany Crescent has done a bit to stimulate activity," grinned Ross MacAllister.

The tall, lean man in the doorway of the office called out to them, "Bill Franks. Night Editor. Come in."

Like most of his staff, he had his jacket off and his sleeves rolled high, with his collar open. In spite of the frantic activity, he seemed amicable.

"A pleasant surprise, Superintendent," smiled Franks. "It's not often the police call on us—usually it's the other way round."

"I agree—you call on us when you want help. Now I'm calling on you when I want help," and there was a cheeky light in Hamilton's eyes.

"Pleased to be of assistance. I take it you're referring to the Dowd murder?"

"I am, Mr. Franks. We want to know more about Hannah Dowd—as much as we can—about her past life, her present life, her associates, her movements. Anything that will give us a lead."

"And why come here?"

"Because you will surely have a file about her—a famous actress."

"Ah, yes. Of course. Annette Wallace, fading star of stage and screen. Yes, indeed. As a matter of fact, we're compiling a feature article about her for tomorrow's *Post*."

"Have I access to your file?"

"If you promise to give us the scoop—if there is a scoop!"

"I'll phone you first with any news—before the sharks who are waiting outside Albany Crescent get to hear of it. You have my word, Mr. Franks."

"Good. I'm ready for a cup of tea. How about you?"

"Never say no."

"Good. I'll fix that, and you can have a peek at our cuttings file on Mrs. Dowd. Not a lot to tell, really, but you might find something."

"Thanks."

Bill Franks was as good as his word. He brought back a tray full of cups and a teapot, and settled down beside them.

"Any news yet?"

"Not yet. We're following one or two leads, but so far—nothing."

"Good. Well, here's the file."

A junior reporter brought in the file of cuttings, large and unwieldy, and placed it on their table.

"Help yourselves, gentlemen. Mind if

I leave you? I've got work to do. This place is all go."

"Thanks. We'll be fine." And Bill Franks left them.

"I want to know," Hamilton told the others, "where she went in her spare time. The neighbours don't know much about her, and she spends a lot of time away from home."

"But if she takes in lodgers..."

"Exactly, Mr. MacAllister," said Hamilton. "But are we sure they are lodgers? That list of names might be something else, mightn't it? The lodgers might, in fact, have been, say, family? Friends? Customers?" He emphasized the last word.

"You mean *she* might have been pushing dangerous drugs?" Gwyn Thomas seemed incredulous at the suggestion.

"Why not?"

"No reason at all, sir. But it seems odd that no one suspected her before."

"Maybe she was very clever. But first,

let's get to work on this pile of paper. We'll see what we can deduce from this."

They waded through, each taking a portion of the file, and their duty was to eliminate the rubbish and take note of useful facts. This wasn't easy—was an alleged affair with another actor a useful fact? Did the fact that she once bought a pair of racehorses matter to the enquiry? Her own family—mother, father, brothers and sisters? Where were they? Who were they?

And so it went on, fact after fact, with one or two suggested scandals thrown in.

Hamilton nodded and shook his head, indicating what he wanted to keep and what they should ignore.

She had a country house in Buckinghamshire—Rock House—at a place called Quarton. That was important! She had had three husbands—the latest, Henry Dowd had died in the last war and there was one child—a daughter called Pauline, by that marriage.

"Hey, sir. Look at this. Her first husband—he was called Hewitt!"

"Hewitt?"

They read the cutting. It recounted the wedding of the actress, Anette Wallace, to a businessman from Manchester, called Ernest Hewitt in 1926. She was then twenty-eight, and at the height of her fame. . . .

"Eric Hewitt, sir. The dead man in Leeds. . . ."

"A son, eh?" suggested Hamilton.

"This is the sort of stuff we need, sir," said Gwyn Thomas. "These actresses sometimes lead queer lives . . ."

The inquisition continued.

Snippets were gathered, gossip was noted. Hamilton's notebook grew as page after page was filled with his untidy scrawl, jotting down all snippets which might help. Details of her trips abroad; her parties, her wild and famous friends.

But one curious thing emerged. There was very little, if no mention of her home in Albany Crescent. Even for a local paper like the *Birmingham Mail* there seemed significantly little note of her life in this locality.

Hamilton spotted this, and signalled for Bill Franks.

He came immediately, willing to help because he recognized the makings of a first class story.

"Yes?"

"I'm rather curious about one thing, Mr. Franks. Although this woman is a local celebrity, there's practically no mention of that fact in these cuttings. They relate to her life as a famous person —all the gaiety, glamour, parties, gossip —it's all society column stuff, or garish news stories. No local stuff."

"Point taken, Superintendent. We had noticed this ourselves—in fact, we didn't really consider her as a local celebrity, and even when she was found dead, we didn't see the connection. But a member of our staff remembered a snippet somewhere and it was only then that our men realized who she really was. A relation of hers had let it slip, but we didn't pay much attention at the time. After all, she was nobody then."

"But one of my staff knew her as Annette Wallace?"

"Your Chief Inspector. We told him."

"Good. Well, any ideas why this happened? Why should she live in such an ordinary house when she had such wonderful properties elsewhere—if your cuttings are accurate she has a beautiful place in Buckinghamshire and a house on the Mediterranean coast."

"This is the angle we've adopted for the feature article about her in tomorrow's *Post*. We'll probably give it a mention in the *Evening Mail* too. We've done a lot of telephoning and interviewing today—you can well imagine—and it seems she liked to lead a double life. In Buckinghamshire—or abroad—she was a fine, wealthy person—an ex-actress of fame and distinction. In those fine homes, she lived that life to the full—the life of a rich person with parties, famous guests and all the trappings of splendour and money. Then she came here, to Albany Crescent. A plain, ordinary person who kept a dingy house used by boarders. No one connected the two lives. No one. When she went away from any of her homes, no one knew where she went. You see, Superintendent, you see how her two lives just did not mix? They were miles apart."

"I do. I see it very clearly. Has she always behaved like this?"

"It seems she has. One reason may be that she came from a very ordinary background. Working class people, and—you'll find this in one of the articles in that file—she liked their warmth and friendliness, their lack of pretentiousness. So she came back to live among them, whenever she could. Anonymously almost, except for a few close friends and relatives. No one outside those people knew who she was."

"But she had to maintain her high life and grand homes for professional reasons?"

"That's about it—mind you, Superintendent, this is only a theory on our part, but having regard to everything we've unearthed, I think it is a feasible one."

"I agree with you, Mr. Franks."

"Have you found anything interesting?"

"Bits and pieces. We're hoping to find trace of relatives and so on. Children—we think she had two daughters."

"She has. One lives in Australia—Canberra in fact."

"You know all about it?"

"Oh, you're one up on us. She'll have to be told. . . . I'll ring our office and ask them to get in touch with Canberra police. Got her address?"

"Sure. Now or later?"

"Oh, later I think. What about the other daughter?"

"Killed in a road accident. . . ."

"A road accident?" the intonation was clear in Hamilton's voice.

"Some years ago, as a young girl. Coming home from a dance with a crowd of youngsters in a car. Failed to take a bend and crashed. Mildred—Milly—was killed."

"Who was Milly's father?"

"Hewitt."

"And her sons?"

"We don't know about those, I'm afraid. Do you?"

"Not with any certainty. I'll help you there if I can."

"You know, Superintendent, I've a feeling you know a little more than you admit."

"But you know I'll never admit that, don't you?" returned Hamilton with a chuckle deep in his chest.

"Yes. Well, press on." And Bill Franks returned to his task of getting the night's work edited and presented for the morning's edition.

Hamilton continued to jot down snippets from the file, but he was flipping through the pages with more abandon now. He had read and digested all the comparatively modern information about Annette Wallace; the rest was pre-war stuff, mostly at the height of her fame. And then, as today, there was nothing to connect her with Edgbaston, or anywhere in the Birmingham area. These were simply interesting news items of a famous star.

At four forty-five, Hamilton stopped.

"I think I've got enough," he announced to his companions. "We know where to come if there's some more."

He rose and went across to Mr. Franks, hard at work on the day's copy, and thanked him. He reiterated his promise to give him any possible scoop, then left the office.

"Come on," he said, "back to Albany Crescent. I've got a lot of telephoning to do."

Gwyn Thomas looked at Ross and Kilby who both nodded. They were beginning to tire now. The length and pace of the day's events were having an effect upon them all.

Gwyn Thomas spoke in the car, "So we think Eric Hewitt is a son by a previous marriage, sir. We haven't solved the problem of the York victim yet."

"I'm backing 'another son', possibly by the same father. In the meantime, I want the Buckinghamshire police to go to her house down there and ask a few questions. We may learn something about her from that end. I think we can rule the daughters out. Did you see the photo of the wedding among those cuttings?"

"I didn't," admitted Gwyn Thomas.

"I spotted it," chirruped Hamilton. "A copy of that one we found in the house. Remember? The girl was her daughter—the one in Canberra. And the man Ross MacAllister has seen in York mortuary was standing next to her—her son, I'll warrant. Best man at the wedding . . . we need proof though. Proof. What else was there?"

"Her movements—holidays."

"Buckinghamshire might help establish that. There'll be friends and contacts down there. Society class."

"Can we rely on them to make a thorough job?" asked Gwyn Thomas. "There's nothing like personal contact, you know."

"Fancy a trip to Buckinghamshire, Inspector?"

"Wouldn't say no, sir. After all, it's all in an effort to get our crime solved."

"You have photos, haven't you? You

must show them to the staff of the house in Buckinghamshire—it's in a village called Quarton."

"Oh, yes."

"How about you, Sergeant Kilby?"

"I'd better get home to Leeds, sir. My body is almost identified—I can do a lot from my home territory now."

"Right. I'll have a car take you home. What about you, MacAllister?"

"I haven't told Maureen where I am. What time is it?"

"Nearly five o'clock."

"And how long to Quarton?"

"Couple of hours at the outside."

"I'll ring Maureen from there," said Ross MacAllister.

"Good. I'll organize a car."

"Buckinghamshire, here we come," said Inspector Gwyn Thomas.

"I'm going to bed," muttered Sergeant Kilby, "in Leeds!"

10

ROCK HOUSE, Quarton, proved to be a large detached house set in its own grounds, with rose gardens, beautifully laid lawns and trellis work. It lay on the outskirts of the village.

Hamilton drew up outside and looked at his watch.

"Half-past seven," he said. "A bit early to start asking questions."

"I fancy a leg stretch," said Ross.

"Then let's go for a walk."

With that, Superintendent Hamilton turned the car around, and parked it on a stretch of waste ground a few yards away from the house.

Being security minded, he locked all the doors and the three men perambulated through the quiet village streets. Hamilton took this opportunity to talk about the case; talking led to new ideas, theories.

"The suspects from that house, Ross." He was now using MacAllister's Christian name freely. "No sign of them yet. We've got an 'All Stations' alert for them; so we should come across them somewhere."

"We're not much nearer to identifying my man in York, are we?" put in Gwyn Thomas.

"Not really. But we'll see what happens at this house when I show a photograph or two to the staff."

"That might help."

"Do you think drugs could be the motive, Inspector Thomas? Is it feasible?"

"I don't know, sir. I can think of nothing else, but there's no doubt that the identification of our road accident victims will help. Are they family or not? If they are, it might be a family killing. Money involved; insurance, or even property. Some kinky relative bumping off all and sundry to get his hands on a bit of wealth."

"I agree. But what relative? So far we

haven't had much luck in tracing relatives, have we?"

"No, but the killing isn't very old. It's only a few hours since it happened and these things take time."

"I appreciate that. Let's suppose, for the time being, they are all one family—and remember this is highly likely—let's suppose they are sons, or something. Where do we go next? Abandon the drugs line of enquiry?"

"It would seem advisable, sir," said Gwyn Thomas without much conviction in his voice. "Surely that suggests a family feud or something."

Ross MacAllister spoke up, "It could mean both, couldn't it? A family involved in drug pushing . . . it's not impossible."

Hamilton strolled along with his fat hands clenched behind his broad back. "You've hit a possibility, Ross. A very distinct possibility. . . ."

Gwyn Thomas said, "Has he? I wouldn't think so!" The Welsh in his voice came out very strongly. "Either we follow the drugs line—and I think that is a good idea, or we follow the family line. Hardly both. Drugs could provide a powerful motive, sir."

"And so could family wealth, Inspector. So could family wealth—look at this house—large, expensive—it'll cost a packet to run the place. There's money tied up in that house, you know. And she has one overseas too."

"Plus one in Edgbaston," chipped in Ross MacAllister.

"Yes, plus one in Edgbaston," echoed Superintendent Hamilton. "So she's not exactly a pauper."

"You've got someone looking up Somerset House records, so I suggest we exhaust enquiries here, sir," advised Gwyn Thomas. "Let's see what we unearth at this house."

"Yep. Let's see what we learn here. Ross—you haven't phoned your wife yet."

Ross glanced at his watch. "Nearly eight o'clock. She'll be getting the kids off to school. I wonder if there's a kiosk around here?"

"Should be one somewhere in the place."

They continued their stroll, admiring the architecture of the village, the layout of the houses, the quiet freshness of early morning, and the pleasing air of serenity.

"Kiosk over there, Ross," pointed Gwyn Thomas, indicating a telephone booth a hundred yards ahead of them.

"I'll ring now."

"Got enough cash?"

"I'll reverse the charges—I'm paying anyway!"

As Ross made his call, the others wandered slowly away, heads down and deep in thought.

It took a while for Ross to get a connection with his home number, and eventually Maureen answered. He was cut off momentarily as the operator asked if she would accept a reverse charge call from Mr. Ross MacAllister, and when she agreed, he was put through.

"Maureen?"

"Ross, is that you? Oh, I've been so worried! Did you come home?"

"No, darling. Sorry. I should have rung last night but didn't have time. I expect to be back sometime today—can't say when."

"But where are you? You sound an awful long way off."

"Buckinghamshire," he said casually. "A little place called Quarton."

"Quarton? Never heard of it. What on earth are you doing there? I thought you'd gone to York to make a statement."

"I did. I've been in Birmingham all night, and now I'm down here with Gwyn Thomas."

"Ross MacAllister! Why can't you leave things alone? Why must you always get so involved in everything that comes your way?"

"Hush, old girl! We're wasting money. Look. I'll be home today sometime. Probably teatime."

"Oh, all right. I'll have something hot for you."

"And enough water for a bath, darling—you can rub my back if you like!"

"I'll rub more than your back, Ross MacAllister! Now hurry home and . . ."

"Yes?"

"Please be careful, Ross."

"Always am. 'Bye, darling."

"'Bye."

He rejoined his colleagues in the street and they decided to return to Rock House. It was nearly ten past eight—it would be twenty-past by the time they reached the house.

Superintendent Hamilton led the way through the open iron gates. Their feet crunched on the gravel drive as they strode between the lawns and flowered borders.

Gwyn pointed.

"Door round the side," he said, "under that glass canopy."

Beneath the canopy a stone flagged path ran beside a large room and an old-fashioned bell-pull showed in the wall adjoining the door.

"Looks lived-in," commented Hamilton, pulling the bell. It clanged in the hall and was answered by a tiny figure in a black dress.

"Good morning," began Hamilton.

The little old lady bowed slightly. She had a round face with rimless spectacles and a florid complexion typical of a country person. "Good morning, sir. Won't you step inside."

"Thank you," and Hamilton was followed by Gwyn Thomas and Ross MacAllister.

"Er, we are police officers," announced Hamilton who automatically assumed the role of spokesman, "from Birmingham."

"I see," nodded their quaint little host.

"It's about your mistress."

"She's away, sir. Miss Wallace is away from home for a while. I don't know when she will be returning."

Hamilton swallowed visibly and gave a sideways glance at his companions.

"Er, I'm here to say she won't be returning . . . er . . . what is your name?"

"Mavis, sir."

"Mavis, eh. Well, Mavis. Miss Wallace

has had a nasty accident, and, I'm afraid . . ."

Mavis had her hand across her mouth. "Oh," she stifled a sob, "oh, no!" And she began to wring her hands.

Hamilton found it hard going. "She's dead, Mavis. Your mistress is dead."

Mavis had a handkerchief over her mouth now, gazing in horror at the man who brought such awful news to Rock House.

"She was murdered, Mavis." Now Hamilton was being brutal, but it was the only way. "Yesterday lunchtime. In her house at Edgbaston."

Mavis stood still without saying a word, then turned and ran from the entrance hall, sobbing aloud now. The sound of her anguish filled the large house and echoed around their ears.

Then another woman appeared; an efficient matronly type with hair pulled tight about her head in a bun. A woman about forty. A spinster without any doubt.

"What is it?" she demanded sharply.

"To whom am I speaking, madam?" asked Hamilton.

"My name is Joan Edwards. Miss Joan Edwards." She emphasized the Miss. "I am Annette Wallace's private secretary."

"You live here?"

"On the premises. All the time, unless I accompany Miss Wallace abroad."

"I see. Did you hear the news I passed to Mavis?"

"No. But who are you? You look like detectives." Her grey eyes ranged from one to the other.

Hamilton continued, "We are detectives. I am Detective Superintendent Hamilton of Birmingham City police. This is Detective Inspector Gwyn Thomas from York and his friend Ross MacAllister who is helping with this enquiry."

"Oh." Her voice was weaker now. "Oh, that sounds ominous. What's happened? Something's happened to Annette? Something awful!"

And like Mavis, she put her hands to her mouth, waiting; tense and frightened.

"Something awful has happened, Miss Edwards. Your mistress is dead."

"Dead? Oh, no!"

"She was murdered yesterday at Birmingham."

"Murdered. No! God, you can't mean that!"

Joan Edwards sank into a chair against the hall wall, pale but making a determined effort not to break down.

Hamilton allowed her to take her time. She looked at him. "How, Superintendent? How was it done?"

"Violence in her home. A blunt instrument."

"Poor Annette . . . poor soul . . . she was so kind . . . but . . ."

"Yes?"

"Did you say Birmingham?"

"Yes. Birmingham. Forty-two Albany Crescent, Edgbaston, to be precise, Miss Edwards. Her Birmingham address. She doesn't use her stage name there—we know her as Mrs. Hannah Dowd, a widow."

The expression on Joan Edwards' face

was a mixture of bewilderment and disbelief. "But, Superintendent, she is away in France . . . I booked the flight myself. From London airport. Four weeks ago!"

"Oh, God!" cried Hamilton. "Don't say that! The file, Inspector. The wedding photographs. Show them to Miss Edwards."

"Look, you'd better all come into the drawing-room." She stood up, composed but still pale and clearly shaken by Hamilton's words. But her face showed hope—hope that the dead person was not, after all, her mistress.

"Sit down, please."

She took a chair near a drop leaf table and Gwyn Thomas went across to her with the wedding photograph in his hand.

He pointed to the group.

"We think the wedding is that of Mrs. Dowd's daughter," he explained. "And we think this girl, and her husband, now live in Canberra, Australia."

Joan Edwards was weeping softly now.

She nodded her head. "She has a girl out there."

"And this," pointed Gwyn, "is this Mrs. Dowd."

Again, Joan Edwards nodded slowly, making no attempt to stifle her tears.

"It looks like her . . . it looks like her. She never told me about Birmingham!"

"You all right, Miss Edwards?" Hamilton came across the room.

"Yes. Yes, I'm being silly. Is there someone else on the picture you want me to see?" She was cold and efficient now. There was no emotion.

Gwyn pointed to the best man. "Who is this?"

"Her eldest son, George."

"George Dowd?"

"No, Wallace. George Wallace."

"By her first marriage?"

"I don't know. She never talked about her early days to me. Maybe she wasn't married when George was born."

"Did he come here at all?"

She nodded. "Quite a lot. Week-ends, when she was at home. Sometimes during mid-week—but I rarely saw him."

"Would you be prepared to come to

York to see a body, Miss Edwards. To identify it...."

"But I thought she was at Birmingham, Superintendent?"

"A man was run down and killed by a car in York yesterday, Miss Edwards. We have reason to believe it was George Wallace."

"Oh, no! Oh, no!" And she collapsed into a flood of tears on the table, cradling her head in her arms and sobbing mercilessly. Hamilton was shocked at her sudden collapse—was she in love with George Wallace?

"Ring for Mavis ... call Mavis. Do something," ordered Hamilton. "A good stiff drink even ..."

Ross MacAllister left the room and shouted, "Mavis ..."

She appeared in a jiffy.

"Sir?" And then she saw Miss Edwards; without a word she moved across to the distressed woman. "There, there." And Mavis ministered to her colleague.

Gradually, the presence of little Mavis

had its effect, and Hamilton decided not to mention the possibility of the death of another son at Leeds.

"Had she any more children?"

Joan Edwards wiped her reddened eyes and nodded. "By her second marriage. A son called Eric—Eric Hewitt. We don't see much of him I'm afraid. I don't know him."

Hamilton looked across at Gwyn Thomas who shook his head; the message was understood. Besides, Kilby had taken his file back to Leeds, so they couldn't get an identification by photograph.

"Now, Miss Edwards," continued Hamilton, "you said Miss Wallace was abroad. Have you heard from her?"

"A postcard."

"When?"

"Twelve days ago."

"Have you got it?"

Mavis answered, "It's in the staff lounge, sir. I'll bring it."

Mavis returned shortly with the card, posted in Nice a fortnight prior to her death. Mavis quietly left the room.

"I'd like to keep this," requested Hamilton.

Joan Edwards nodded, but didn't ask why. Hamilton wanted to check the handwriting against that found in Albany Crescent.

"Now, Miss Edwards, so far as you are aware, she is still abroad?"

"Yes, oh, yes. Make her be abroad . . . make it be a ghastly mistake. . . ."

"When is she due to return?"

"Tomorrow. Saturday. I was to take a car to London to meet her at three tomorrow afternoon."

"At the airport?"

"No. In town. Outside Claridges actually. I usually meet her there."

"Will you go tomorrow?"

"Of course, Superintendent. So far as I am concerned, my mistress had nothing to do with Birmingham at all. I realize the woman on the photograph is like her, very like her. But it can't be her, can it? Can it?"

"I don't see why not, Miss Edwards. She might have very personal reasons for living in Birmingham anonymously—it's easy to return to Birmingham from abroad, and still meet you outside Claridges."

"But she told me everything. Everything. I booked the flight . . ."

"She could change her mind and return early, you know—providing there was a seat."

"Yes. Yes, but she wouldn't. Not without telling me."

"Did you meet her often outside Claridges in this manner?—after a trip abroad, I mean?"

Joan Edwards nodded. "Two or three times a year. Maybe more."

"Have you the dates? This is important."

"In the desk diary. I made notes so that I wouldn't forget. Superintendent, do you honestly think Annette has been killed?"

"I don't know," admitted Superintendent Hamilton.

11

THE task was not a long one. Joan Edwards, composed and efficient, flipped through the pages of the diary and produced the dates within the past year that she had been to London to collect her mistress.

Each was a Saturday—the 13th January; 9th March; 20th April; 15th June; 7th September and 21st December.

"Thanks. Now, Miss Edwards. Did you cancel any of her seat reservations?"

She shook her head. "But I did book abroad for every one of those periods. If you check with the airline . . ."

"We'll have to. I want to know how many times she went abroad on the tickets you booked. Did, or does, she always send letters or postcards?"

"No. She's terrible. Hardly ever writes."

"Mmm. So either we have the wrong

woman, or your mistress has been leading a very clever double life. Done to deceive even you, Miss Edwards. Are you a friend, apart from being an employee?"

"Yes. A lifelong friend, Superintendent. I know you've got the wrong person—and I must say I'm not sorry!"

Hamilton was non-committal. "Did she always use her stage name when travelling? When you booked seats for her, was it in the name of Annette Wallace?"

"Oh, yes. She never used any other name."

"Thanks. Now, I must search her room—in fact, the entire house. I need some evidence to establish the identity of the dead woman. I must ask your permission, of course, that's only courteous, but we can search without any permission."

"I appreciate that. You may go ahead. I'll take you to her room."

"I would like you to stay with us, Miss Edwards. To guide us around and explain what we find—if we find anything."

"Of course."

The search took well over an hour,

Hamilton worked quickly and thoroughly, inspecting all drawers and cupboards in Annette Wallace's private rooms, the maids' rooms, and Joan Edwards' apartment.

There were the usual items of minor interest—letters, photographs, personal belongings, clothes and press cuttings galore. Press cuttings. Mrs. Dowd had press cuttings, showing Annette Wallace's triumphs. Hamilton made a mental note of that. One woman or two? Was one a devoted fan of the other? A sister?

The house and its contents yielded absolutely no information. It only served to confirm Joan Edwards' story that Annette Wallace was overseas, and nowhere in the house did he find any mention of Edgbaston or Birmingham.

And yet the press had the whole story!

It was almost ten-thirty by the time the search of the house was complete and Hamilton said, "I think my next job is to check with London Airport—to see if the reservations were cancelled for her trips back from Nice. Does she always go to Nice?"

"Yes, always. She has a villa there. Cherry Tree Villa."

Gwyn Thomas spoke, "You could ring Nice through Interpol, sir. Get them to check straightaway."

"I could, Gwyn. But I think I'll check the airport first. Depending on the answer I receive, I'll then check with Nice, maybe. She is due back tomorrow, if Miss Edwards' information is correct."

"Please check, won't you? One way or the other?" Joan Edwards pleaded.

"Yes. Can we use this telephone?"

"Anything," she told them, "anything." She rang a hand bell and Mavis appeared. "Coffee for all of us, Mavis. Milk and sugar, gentlemen?"

"Please," they chorused, as Hamilton looked up the airport's telephone number.

"I've got the number," Joan Edwards told him. "I keep it in a notebook, along with other useful numbers. You can dial it from here, Superintendent. Ask for extension 304. It puts you direct to the booking clerk."

Hamilton appreciated her knowledge and dialled carefully. He was through in a few moments.

"Extension 304," he requested.

A few clicks, and he was connected with one of the booking clerks.

"This is Detective Superintendent Hamilton, Birmingham City police," he announced. "I have an enquiry about the possible cancellation of several seat reservations dating back some months. Can you help me?"

"Yes, sir. Go ahead. Under what name were the bookings made."

"Annette Wallace, of Quarton, in Buckinghamshire, and the dates are as follows . . ."

He paused and she said, "I'll take them down."

Hamilton gave the list of dates he'd got from Joan Edwards, and explained that the cancellations would be on the incoming flights from Nice on the dates he gave. He also asked if there had been journeys into London from Nice shortly before the given dates. He explained that such trips might be in the name of either Annette Wallace or Hannah Dowd.

The girl appeared to have grasped the gist of his enquiry and asked him to hang on for a few minutes.

"We have an index of passengers for each month," she explained, "in alphabetical order. It's not a long job to check the names against the dates the flights were made."

"I can wait."

Joan Edwards hung about, close to Hamilton, waiting, nervous. She was silent. As they waited, Mavis arrived with a percolator of coffee and some cups. They took a cup each as Mavis left them.

Then Hamilton responded to the telephone; the girl was back. "Hello."

"I'm still here."

"The name Wallace, Superintendent. I have checked on the dates you mentioned. There was no cancellation on those dates. The reservations were taken—they were the return journeys of earlier flights made to Nice."

"On each of the dates I gave you?"

"Yes. In every case. And, as a matter of interest, the same lady is returning from Nice tomorrow."

"Then you've received no cancellation for tomorrow?"

"No, sir."

"Thank you. Now, did you check on the name of Dowd, Hannah Dowd?"

"Yes. I did. The name does appear one week before the return trip of the Wallace woman in every case. One week earlier."

"Really? A single trip—Nice to London?"

"Yes. A single trip."

"Thank you. And the most recent Dowd arrival? It should have been last Saturday then?"

"Yes. It was. The noon arrival from Nice. Mrs. Hannah Dowd."

"This is wonderful news. Now, I shall need a formal statement of evidence from you. Can I arrange for an airport policeman to visit you? What is the best time?"

The girl seemed quite unabashed by the demands of Superintendent Hamilton and he guessed she'd had this type of enquiry before; no doubt Scotland Yard made frequent checks on the passenger lists.

"I'm here every day between eight-thirty and five," she said. "And I will make a statement. The airport policeman knows the routine about seeking permission from my superiors and so on."

"I'll arrange that. Good-bye and thank you."

He replaced the receiver, but Joan Edwards was near him, her face showing curiosity and anxiety.

"I heard what you said," she whispered. "No flights cancelled. I told you she was abroad, I told you. It's someone else."

"And the Mrs. Dowd who comes in a week before Annette Wallace: Who is she?"

"Oh dear, this is terrible . . . terrible

... shall I send a telegram to Nice, Superintendent? I must find out."

"I can't allow that, I'm afraid. Not now, in the light of recent developments. What are your arrangements for meeting the lady tomorrow?"

"The same as usual. I don't meet the plane—it arrives at noon. I drive down to London and meet Annette outside Claridges at three in the afternoon."

"The luggage? What about that?"

"She has always had it sent here by rail. She carries one case—no more."

"Good. Now I want you to go to London tomorrow as arranged, but I do not want any sort of contact with Nice. I want to see who gets off the plane tomorrow on Annette Wallace's reservation. And, Miss Edwards, I want you to see the body at Birmingham."

"Me? Oh, I couldn't."

"So far as we are aware, you are the only person who can tell us whether or not the dead woman at Birmingham is Annette Wallace, alias Hannah Dowd. I must insist that you come with us."

"Not now?"

"Now." Hamilton was adopting an unusual firmness with the woman. "I must insist. Then you are free to come home. We will bring you home—at police expense."

"Give me ten minutes to get ready, Superintendent."

When she had gone upstairs, Hamilton said, "Listen for the telephone. I don't want that woman to ring Nice, or anywhere else for that matter. Someone is due to arrive in London tomorrow and I don't want them frightened off."

"Is there an extension to the bedroom?"

"I didn't see one when we were looking around, but one can't be too careful."

Hamilton paced up and down the room of the magnificent house, large moustache bristling as he licked his lips and sucked his teeth. He was thinking hard, ranging across the few certain facts that were in his possession.

"Any idea what's going on, sir?" asked Gwyn Thomas.

"Not yet, Gwyn. Bloody funny though. We must make this woman view the body found at forty-two Albany Crescent."

"She's a bit of a mess, sir. The head's been battered rather nastily."

"All the more reason for the Edwards woman to view it."

Ross MacAllister spoke, "What about the Leeds and York victims, sir? Should she see those?"

"I was thinking along those lines, Ross. Let's play it off the cuff; I want to test her reaction in Birmingham first."

Gwyn Thomas butted in, "Then you're not entirely satisfied with her story."

"I didn't say that, Gwyn. . . . Ah! Footsteps."

Joan Edwards appeared carrying a large handbag, and she was dressed in a smart blue suit with matching shoes and gloves. A smart, attractive woman, but one without any man-appeal. Cold and hard, thought Ross.

"You'll have me back by teatime, will you?"

"Of course," said Hamilton. "We

should be in Birmingham shortly after one o'clock. We'll get some lunch and then get down to our unpleasant task. You should be home by four-thirty, Miss Edwards."

"Thank you."

They left Mavis in charge of the house; Hamilton was satisfied that Mavis knew little or nothing about the events and would not inform anyone in Nice. She probably didn't know how to use a telephone, anyway.

Joan Edwards settled herself in the rear of the car, composed and friendly, and Ross MacAllister settled down beside her.

Back in Birmingham, there had been little development. The night shift had gone off duty at six o'clock with little to report. After receiving Hamilton's request to search for Rodney Hill and his companions, traffic checks had been set up on all the major roads leading from the city, and the night duty detectives had carried out a systematic search of Hill's known haunts, all without result.

They had also searched the haunts of other known drug addicts and their like within the boundaries of the City, and although they had made a few unspectacular arrests for drug offences, Hill and his colleagues had escaped their vigilance.

All this was reported back to Detective Inspector Crispin, second in charge of the murder enquiry at Albany Crescent. He noted it all in the dossier.

Apart from the routine work of the investigation, there had been few leads or successful lines to follow. Mrs. Dowd seemed to be practically unknown in this area; the neighbours couldn't help, except to say she was away from home a lot.

There seemed to be no real scandal attached to her life, and Crispin noted the report of the death in the morning's *Birmingham Post*. It said very little.

It merely recorded the death of Mrs. Hannah Dowd, who was better known under her stage name of Annette Wallace, a secret she had maintained in Edgbaston. The report added that police were investigating the death. An obituary of Mrs.

Dowd, giving her full credit under the name of Annette Wallace was printed elsewhere in the paper with a brief résumé of her career. A footnote added that a dedication would be made in the *Evening Post*.

In Crispin's mind, this publicity might be beneficial—people would recall the woman and remember incidents. Already, teams of detectives aided by the uniform branch, were out in Birmingham on the tedious chore of house-to-house enquiries, and all the shopkeepers and tradesmen with whom she dealt, or who called at the house, were being interviewed.

Crispin found himself acting more as an administrator than a working detective, but administrators were needed to collate the facts. He was receiving the mass of written statements, and had a staff of four to cope with the written work and the mass of calls which came through the temporary telephone now installed at Albany Crescent.

But most of the statements were negative. They told very little.

Crispin had a horrible feeling that this was going to develop into an unsolved murder. He hoped that Leeds and York police had better luck with their side of the enquiry.

In York, little had been done due to the absence of Inspector Thomas in Birmingham, but Police Constable Watkins, the man who had visited the scene, was busy with his paper work. Last night, he had witnessed the post mortem examination, when the Pathologist, Doctor Woodford, confirmed that death was due to multiple injuries and shock.

Watkins, a seasoned policeman, had telephoned the local Coroner this morning, and the inquest would be postponed until an identifying witness could be found.

The body could be kept in a refrigeration plant. Watkins now awaited the return of his superior officers. There was little more he could do.

In the meantime, he dealt with the

mundane work of preparing an accident report, with sketches. This was necessary for every road accident, large or small. And, even though other factors were involved, this was basically a fatal road accident and, as such, would warrant a figure "1" in the annual Home Office statistics of road accidents.

Watkins worked slowly. He wasn't an office man—he was a practical bobby, but the writing of the report was his job. No one could do it for him.

Similar work was being done in Leeds City. Detective Sergeant Kilby had returned late last night, and, consequently, hadn't turned up at the office by nine o'clock.

But by ten-thirty, he was in his chair. He gave his Inspector an account of the developments and even then, it took a sound argument to convince the Inspector that their hit-and-run incident was in fact a murder. But once he was convinced, he took immediate action.

Armed with photographs of the deceased man, believed to be Eric Hewitt, teams of detectives began urgent and concise enquiries from hotels and boarding houses in Leeds.

The press was told; the Yorkshire *Evening Post* reporter went along for the story which was linked with the York City accident—linked by coincidence and no more. But the press would make a meal of it.

It was hoped that the press accounts would produce someone in Leeds who had seen Hewitt.

At the Birmingham Police mortuary, Superintendent Hamilton escorted Joan Edwards into the cold, shivery interior. A policewoman hovered discreetly nearby in case of fainting attacks, or other trouble, and Hamilton pushed open the plain wooden doors.

A white coated attendant came forward to meet them and Hamilton said, "The body from Albany Crescent, please."

The attendant nodded and walked across to a massive refrigeration plant in which were huge drawers. It was like a massive filing cabinet.

Without a word, he drew out one of the drawers and removed a white shroud from the figure it contained.

"Right," was all he said.

"Ready?" Hamilton asked Miss Edwards.

She nodded, and he saw that she was pale, nervous. Frightened?

He took her arm and said softly, "This is never pleasant, Miss Edwards. Take a steady look at her. Don't be frightened, and then tell me if this is Annette Wallace —the woman you know."

"I'm all right," she said bravely, and Hamilton found she was gripping his arm fiercely. "Let's get it over."

He took her to the drawer, exposed at waist height, and she looked down at the battered corpse. The bruise across the eye on the right; the abrasions on the cheeks, the washed wounds. The fractured skull didn't show among the mass of greying hair; the blood had been cleaned away.

"Well?" asked Hamilton.

Joan Edwards looked at him and said, "That isn't her, Superintendent. That isn't Annette Wallace."

12

"ARE you sure?" Hamilton didn't sound surprised. He put the question as a matter of course, for he wanted the woman to have another look. She obliged without thinking.

"I'm sure, Superintendent. It's like her . . . so like her. But that is not my mistress. I'd swear it."

"Mmm." Hamilton said nothing. "That puts the cat among the pigeons, doesn't it? Who is it then? Any idea? Sister? Relative?"

"I . . . I don't know. Please take me out of here."

"Yes. Yes, of course. Sorry."

Hamilton was like all seasoned policemen—death and the stench of mortuaries meant little to him and he was quite content to chat and ask questions in here.

The mortuary attendant opened the

doors and the fresh air was like nectar to her lungs; it swept away the odours that went with death. The disinfectant, the sickly stenches. The horror.

"I'd like you to come to my office, please," Hamilton said, "to sign a statement to the effect that the woman in there is not Hannah Dowd."

"I'll say it isn't Annette Wallace," she said. "I don't know anyone by the name Hannah Dowd."

"Of course. Silly of me."

He led the way to Police Headquarters and took her into his well appointed office.

"Sit down. I won't be a moment. I've got to find a statement form." He left her alone as he disappeared along the corridor and Joan Edwards sat composed and unsmiling; her face expressionless and her demeanour was one of resigned obedience.

Hamilton returned shortly with some foolscap sheets of paper.

"We must have the right form for everything." He smiled suddenly at her.

"We're getting worse than the Civil Service. As a start, I'll need your full name and address, please."

"Joan Edwards," she said flatly, "Rock House, Quarton, Buckinghamshire."

He was writing quickly as she talked. "Occupation?"

"Secretary, I suppose."

"Good enough for me. Age. I won't ask you that."

"I don't mind," she said. "I'm forty-one."

"You don't look it," he smiled again, and she responded with a flutter of her eyelashes.

"Now then," he said, "all we have to write down is that at two o'clock this afternoon, you saw the body of a woman in Birmingham Police mortuary, in the company of Detective Superintendent Hamilton—that's me—then we need the fact that you can say with certainty that it was not the body of your mistress, Annette Wallace. How's that?"

"Yes, that's right."

He wrote down her words, quickly and

neatly, and then said, "There's a printed certificate at the bottom of these forms, Miss Edwards. It's a new idea—came into being on 1st January 1968, under the Criminal Justice Act 1967—it has got to be signed by you."

"What's it for?"

"It's a declaration of truth—people put all sorts of false stories into statements because they aren't on oath. But this has the same effect as an oath. If we find someone who has made any falsehood in a statement like this, we can take them to court for perjury. It's a useful provision, especially in things like motoring accidents when everybody involved tells huge lies to get the other chap blamed."

"Do I have to sign it?" Again she was calm and unflustered.

"Everyone who makes a statement must sign it." He looked at her earnestly, but she was undaunted.

"Well, I'm telling the truth, if that's what's worrying you."

He shoved the statement and a ballpoint pen across the desk; she read the words he'd written on her behalf, and the printed declaration at the bottom. Finally she signed her name with a flourish.

"Thank you. You've left us with a problem, you know, but there's one more thing before you leave us. I have two photographs I would like you to see please."

"Photographs?"

"Yes. Two men." He pressed the intercom on his desk. "Send in the photographs of the accident fatalities of York and Leeds, will you? They're in the Albany Crescent murder file."

He replaced the speaker and said to her, "Two men were killed by hit-and-run motoring accidents yesterday at twelve-thirty in the afternoon. Both at the same time, and yet over twenty miles apart. One at Leeds and the other at York. I mentioned the York one earlier. Two men. Neither had any means of identification on him, and, up to now, we haven't identified them officially. But one of them—the York man—had a visiting card with Mrs. Dowd's address on it. So we went to ask for her help—and found her dead, too."

"Good gracious!" She clasped her hands before her; taut and slightly nervous.

"Naturally, we feel there is a connection between the three killings—and we think the road accidents weren't simple accidents."

"I follow," she said weakly.

"So we must make every effort to identify the men concerned . . . ah!"

His door opened and a plain clothes man entered with a file.

"Thank you, Sergeant. You can wait a moment."

Hamilton passed the first picture across to her; she took it slowly without looking at it.

"It's all right to look at," Hamilton added quietly, and she allowed her eyes to scan the picture.

"Don't know him. I'm sorry." But there was a tremor in her voice.

"Try this one then."

This was the Leeds victim, and the

response was the same. She shook her head emphatically.

"I'm sorry, Superintendent, I'm so sorry . . . you've brought me all this way . . ."

"Nonsense!" he said. "You've been a lot of help, because you've cleared up a lot of doubt in our minds. We know the victim isn't Annette Wallace and that is a help in some ways. Now, are you ready to go back?"

"Yes, quite ready." She stood up.

"I'll get a patrol car to take you home. Can you fix that, Sergeant?"

The sergeant nodded and said, "Yes, sir." After collecting the file of photographs he left the room.

"We'll go down to the entrance hall, Miss Edwards," said Hamilton. "If you'd like to stay for a cup of tea, or something, before going back . . ."

"No. I'd rather be on my way, thank you. I've a lot to do, and it will be teatime when I return."

"Of course."

As they chatted about nothing in

particular, a sleek black car without police signs, eased to a halt in front of the door and Hamilton said, "Your taxi. I'm sorry I shan't be taking you back but duty calls. Thank you for your help."

"Good-bye, Superintendent."

"I might want to speak with your mistress when she returns from Nice tomorrow," he said as she entered the vehicle.

"Ring tomorrow," she said. "After tea will be the best time. She will arrange something."

"I'll do that." He then addressed the driver, "Take Miss Edwards to Quarton, constable. It's in Buckinghamshire—she'll show you the way."

The car drew away and she didn't wave.

She reminded him of a duchess, sitting aloof in her black limousine.

As the car drove away, Hamilton returned to his office and buzzed for Gwyn Thomas and Ross MacAllister. They came in, anxious to know what had transpired.

"She can't identify our corpse, except to say it is not her mistress. She says she doesn't know who the two men are. Personally, I don't believe her. So what do we do now, gentlemen?"

"I know what I'd do," said Gwyn Thomas, in his lilting accent.

"Tell me."

"I'd have words with the GPO security and have her outgoing and incoming telephone calls bugged. I'd want to know if she was in contact with Nice—or anywhere else for that matter—and I'd want to know what she said."

"You don't trust her, Inspector Thomas?"

"It's not exactly that, sir, but this is a murder enquiry, and in my mind, that woman is now number one suspect."

"Really? What else would you do?"

"Have a first class detective tail her to London tomorrow. Didn't she say she was due to meet Annette Wallace outside Claridges?"

"She did. And if Annette Wallace turns up, Inspector?"

"We interview Annette Wallace."

"And if she doesn't?"

"We take that woman in for further questioning."

"Yes," murmured Hamilton, "yes. Number one suspect, eh? You serious about that?"

"Who else, sir? Damn it all, everyone else seems to be sure that Hannah Dowd and Annette Wallace are the same person. . . . Miss Edwards could easily be lying for her own reasons. Look at it this way—Joan Edwards has been a lifelong friend and companion of the once famous Annette Wallace; Annette Wallace is a widow, with children . . ."

"Do we know that?"

"I'm assuming this for the sake of my argument, sir. Children. She has children and those children will, one assumes, inherit that marvellous house at Quarton, plus all her other wealth."

"Go on, Inspector."

"Our Miss Edwards, being a good secretary and all that, knows about this.

She knows the children and has them destroyed."

"The man at Leeds? The two sons?"

"There's a daughter, though, out in Australia."

"Couldn't the same thing happen out there, sir? An accident . . ."

Hamilton went pale. Australia! He'd not realized the danger out there!

"And so Joan Edwards is left as friend, guide and counsellor. So the fortune goes to her. The house she's used all these years, the villa in Nice, the money . . . And doubtless she thinks she's earned it. Perhaps she's been cut out of the will. . . ."

"I see your point. The will would have to say that the estate was to be divided between all parties, or to the sole survivor. . . ."

"Yes. Dispose of the sons. Mother still alive."

"So all belongs to mother—with a clause which gives everything to the secretary."

"So all the secretary has to do is to

dispose of the mother and it's all hers. The lot."

"Except for the daughter in Australia."

"Get me the file," shouted Hamilton, "and that wedding photograph—I want the married name of the daughter out there. I'll ring Australia House and have a check made on their address. It'll be in their immigration files."

"And a tail on her?"

"Yes. And a tail on her. Buckinghamshire can do that job for us, and I'll fix things with the GPO regarding the telephone."

"Should we bring her back?" put in Ross MacAllister. "You can catch the driver by radio."

Hamilton shook his head. "No grounds, have we? No. Let her go and we'll see what she does next. If she is involved somehow, she'll show us. She'll think she's got away with it, won't she?"

"But the body, sir . . . the woman in the morgue?" asked Ross.

"If our guesswork is correct, Ross, Miss Edwards has lots of good reasons for saying she doesn't know our victims, hasn't she?"

"She has, I suppose. She leaves us with a weighty problem to sort out while she . . ."

"While she makes hay as the sun is shining, eh?" chuckled Hamilton. "Yes. She might be our woman, but we need evidence—and a motive that will stand up in court. I can see what she could gain from the deaths, but we need to know Annette Wallace's solicitors. They'll give us an accurate picture."

"They should not be difficult to trace," said Gwyn Thomas. "The newspapers will help again. If we look through the reports of her divorces, they'll surely contain the names of her solicitors."

"Yep. Good idea. I'll do that next. Now, I must ring Buckinghamshire, and the GPO. Do you fellows want to go home yet?"

"Not on your life," said Ross MacAllister, "this is getting interesting."

The enquiries from Somerset House,

which had been undertaken by the Yard at the request of Hamilton, revealed that a Hannah Briggs had, in fact, been married in 1919 at the age of twenty-one to a man called William Wallace, to whom she bore a son, George. He was born in 1922. When she was twenty-six, she divorced Wallace, and two years later, in 1926, she married a man called Ernest Hewitt. To him, in 1927, she had a son called Eric and four years after their marriage, she divorced Hewitt. But there had been another child to that union, a daughter, Alice, who had died in a road accident.

When Hannah was thirty-six, she married again, this time to a man called Henry Dowd. To him she had a daughter, Pauline, rather late in life. Pauline was born in 1936 when her mother was thirty-eight.

"That'll be the one in Australia," said Hamilton, who read further into the telex message to find that Henry Dowd died shortly after the outbreak of war.

So Hannah Dowd, alias Annette

Wallace, a widow with three surviving children had outlived three husbands.

"It's the same woman all right," said Hamilton, "Mrs. Hannah Dowd is the late Annette Wallace. So we know that Joan Edwards is lying."

"We should have arrested her this afternoon on suspicion, sir," put in Gwyn Thomas.

"We've got her under close surveillance, Gwyn. I want more evidence—we need to prove her motive—and I think I'll get that from the woman herself."

The telephone rang, and Hamilton snatched at it.

"Hamilton speaking. Yes? Oh, hello, Garfield. Yes? Good God, man! Why did you let that happen?"

He listened, then said, "Stay there and carry out a search. I'll ring the local police and ask them to help! God, this is awful!"

He replaced the receiver slowly.

"We've dropped a real clanger, gentlemen. She's escaped from the car."

"Escaped?" cried Gwyn Thomas.

"Well, she's got away, run away. Call it what you like. That was PC Garfield, the driver taking her back home. She wanted to go to the lavatory in Warwick. He stopped outside a public convenience to allow her."

"Hadn't much choice, had he?" put in Gwyn Thomas. "She wasn't a prisoner. We hadn't arrested her and Garfield had no reason to watch her movements."

"I agree. Anyway, she didn't come out after a long time, so he got the attendant to see if she was all right."

"And she'd gone?" put in Ross MacAllister.

"Through another exit—into another street. Vanished."

"Is that the evidence you needed, sir?" asked Gwyn Thomas. "The evidence to prove her guilt?"

"Put out an All Stations message for her arrest," he said in weary reply.

13

AS Gwyn Thomas arranged an "All Stations" message with Birmingham Information Room on one telephone, the other rang and Hamilton answered it.

"Yes?"

"*Birmingham Post*, sir. It's about Annette Wallace."

"Oh!" Hamilton suddenly perked up. "Who's that speaking?"

"Bill Franks, the Editor."

"Yes. What can I do for you?"

"We published a feature on the death of Annette Wallace in today's issue—did you see it?"

"No, haven't had time. But I've got news for you, Mr. Franks. That woman isn't Annette Wallace—at least that's what her secretary says."

"Rubbish, Superintendent. It is

Annette Wallace. Damn it all—everything fits. . . ."

"Yes, I know. That's what we thought . . . anyway. You rang me. Something wrong?"

"No, far from it, Superintendent. We've had a telephone call from a woman in Birmingham—she wants to speak to you about the murder."

"Oh, why?"

"She read our feature about the death, and then the bit about the police being interested—that was in a news item. She's heard that murder might be involved."

"How?"

"Dunno. Gossip, I expect. That sort of thing soon gets around."

"Who is this woman?"

"A cousin of Hannah Dowd. She's a Mrs. Maud Cummins, who lives at forty-eight Coniston Avenue—a new council estate."

"I know it," said Hamilton, "I'll go and see her. Did she say why she wanted to see me?"

"No, sorry."

"Well, thanks for your help, Mr. Franks. Nice to get assistance from you chaps!"

"How are things going then? Any news of an impending arrest yet?"

"Not yet. I'll let you know when we do produce something newsworthy."

"Thank you." He replaced the telephone.

Hamilton barked across the room to a detective sergeant who was flicking through the growing file on the killing.

"Sergeant! Go and find Detective Inspector Crispin. Tell him about that bloody woman's escape and ask him to breathe down everyone's necks for results. She must be found . . . tell him I've rung Australia House and they are making sure that Mrs. Dowd's daughter is safe—we don't like family killings like this in England. And tell him Warwickshire police are keeping an eye open for the Edwards woman."

"Sir," acknowledged the sergeant, who had a clear knowledge of the latest developments.

"And then go along to the *Birmingham Post* and see the editor. I want to know the name of Annette Wallace's solicitors. I'm going to see this Mrs. Cummins. You chaps coming?" he addressed Gwyn Thomas and Ross MacAllister.

They followed him to a car in the yard of the police station and were soon driving through the back streets of Birmingham, avoiding traffic and the congestion of the city.

Within fifteen minutes, Hamilton pulled up outside a neat council house, with a well kept garden and a line of washing hanging outside the back door.

"Forty-eight, the editor said. Next block."

He drove slowly forwards, counting the houses and then stopped outside another house, rather dingy, but clean. The garden was unkempt with long grass and thick weeds.

"She's either got a lazy husband, or a dead one," grunted Hamilton as he clambered out with a deep sigh. "I hope she knows something. Damn! I haven't got the bloody file!"

"I have," said Ross, holding it out, "and it contains a photograph of the Leeds and York victims."

"Thanks. I'm going round in a daze now. I could do with a good sleep."

"All in good time," sympathized Ross. "Think this is genuine?"

"Genuine?" shrieked Hamilton. "Why shouldn't it be genuine?"

"Well, I just wondered," said Ross rather blandly. "Cranks do contact the police when there's a murder in the news."

"I know about that," grumbled Hamilton. "Come along. Let's see what she has to tell us."

They trooped towards the front door of number forty-eight and it opened before they reached it. A pleasant woman, plump and middle-aged with a thick mass of grey hair and a flowered apron, stood in the doorway smiling a welcome.

"You must be police," she said softly.

Hamilton was approaching her. "I am

Detective Superintendent Hamilton," he announced, "and these are two colleagues."

"I am Mrs. Cummins. Please come in; the kettle has just boiled."

They followed her inside; it was a neat council house, tidily and cleanly furnished and she showed them into the living-room.

"Do sit down," she invited, and each man found a seat on the three-piece suite. "Do you all like tea?"

"Please."

"I won't be a moment. I do like to have a cup of tea when I talk," and with that, she pottered through to the kitchen, busy and fussy.

"Seems all right," whispered Gwyn Thomas.

"Just what I thought. Ordinary sort of person. Not the film star type, if you understand."

"Film stars come from ordinary families," pointed out Ross MacAllister. "Nice woman, I think."

They lapsed into silence, and Hamilton

lit his pipe. In the kitchen they heard cups chinking and the sound of a kettle coming to the boil.

"We're not getting very far with this enquiry, lads," Hamilton suddenly said. "I don't seem any further than when I started."

"Oh, I disagree," Gwyn Thomas contradicted. "I think you've got a good suspect in that woman—running away must prove something."

Ross MacAllister joined in, "Don't be too sure of that. Women do some funny things, particularly women who live alone. We've got absolutely nothing to connect her with the Albany Crescent affair, surely."

"Just conjecture, Ross. And the details from Somerset House—they present formidable proof that Mrs. Dowd and Annette Wallace are one and the same person."

"Yes, but that person may be abroad —we might have someone else in our mortuary."

Then the kitchen door opened and they

stopped talking. In came their hostess with a tray of teapots, sugar, milk and buttered scones.

As Mrs. Cummins poured tea and requested them to help themselves, she was saying, "You must be wondering why I tried to get in touch with you."

"It did puzzle us, Mrs. Cummins, particularly as you did it through the *Birmingham Post*."

"I suppose I should have contacted you direct, but I felt a bit shy about coming. The paper had a bit about Hannah, so I rang them."

"You did right, of course. Now, why did you want to speak to us, Mrs. Cummins?"

"Well, I'd heard about the murder, then read the paper. I know the paper didn't say she'd been murdered."

"But she has, I'm afraid," said Hamilton bluntly. "Mrs. Dowd was savagely attacked and we don't know who did it. Nor do we know why. Can you help?"

"I don't know."

"Before you start, Mrs. Cummins, tell me one thing. Are Mrs. Dowd and Annette Wallace one and the same person?"

"Oh, yes, of course . . . she's my cousin, so I should know that, Superintendent."

"Good. Now, perhaps you'll tell us your story. Sorry to have interrupted you."

"That's all right. Well, my mother and Hannah's mother were sisters, and I used to play with her when we were children. She hadn't a gay life, really. Just an ordinary girl from an ordinary home. Well, she got this thing about the stage—about being a dancer and a famous star—even when she was ever so tiny. Well, she worked hard and she did become famous."

"Yes, we knew that," said Hamilton without elaborating on their uncertainty in that direction.

"Well," and Mrs. Cummins dropped her voice, "she got in with the wrong lot . . ."

"The wrong lot?" Hamilton spoke equally quietly.

"The acting profession, you know. Not that I've anything against them, but there are one or two queer people and, well, our Hannah got tangled up with them."

"Has this anything to do with her murder?" He used the word brutally.

Mrs. Cummins nodded. "I think so."

"Please go on. Sorry for the interruptions, but I like to have a clear picture of what's happening."

"That's all right. Well, as I was saying. She got in with the wrong lot. Oh, I know she became famous. She made a lot of money. She had a wonderful time, I suppose, if you like that sort of thing. But the time came for her life of luxury to end."

"You're telling the story very well. Please go on."

"Her name didn't really mean much after the silent films ended—she'd made her name in the old music hall days, and then in the silent films. But her speaking voice didn't win approval in the talkies

. . . she was still young then, really. Young enough to make a good career in the talking pictures, but, well, she didn't."

"So what did she do?"

"She tried all sorts to make money, Mr. Superintendent. All sorts. But she couldn't give up her money, her riches. She couldn't."

Mrs. Cummins began to weep a little, wiping her eye with the corner of her handkerchief.

"Sorry," she sniffed, "it's the thought of it . . . the family disowned her."

"Everyone?"

"Except her own children. They loved her . . . it's only natural, isn't it? They loved her all the time. They didn't know everything, of course. She was so young and they were only children, but when they got older, they found out and . . . well . . . they joined in."

"Joined in what, Mrs. Cummins?"

"Her business ventures. Overseas, mainly. In France . . . other places as well, I think . . . rotten, they were."

"Business ventures? What sort of business?"

"I think the polite word is white-slave traffic." She spoke almost in a whisper.

"Prostitution!" hissed Hamilton. "Prostitution!"

Mrs. Cummins nodded slowly. "Awful, isn't it . . . our Hannah. But she had to keep her lovely house in Buckinghamshire . . . she had to keep up her appearances . . . that's why she did it."

"How did she do it? Was it abroad? How did she get her money back here?"

"I don't know. I think she would advertise in the various film and stage magazines for young girls who were interested in acting careers overseas . . . you know the sort of thing."

"Only too well," admitted Hamilton. "I thought that had died out to a large extent."

"It has . . . it has . . . so . . ." and their informant burst into tears. They welled from her eyes and ran down her plump cheeks. . . . "At least, she got found out once or twice . . . I think the foreign police caught her and found her brothels."

"What did she do?"

"She came back to Albany Crescent—a long time ago."

"How long is a long time, Mrs. Cummins?"

"Fifteen years, perhaps. Maybe more. She used one of her husband's names—Dowd—and kept a boarding house."

"Did you visit her?"

Mrs. Cummins shook her head, "No. But I kept my eyes and ears open. I thought she was being truly well-behaved. I thought she'd abandoned her old ways—then I found out about the house in Buckinghamshire. She kept it going as well; she used to go down there quite often, sometimes for weeks at a time. And she was going abroad."

"Do you know why?"

"The same old thing, Superintendent. She'd started another chain of brothels somewhere abroad. Spain I think, but even worse . . ."

"Worse?"

The unhappy woman was obviously finding it difficult to tell him these unsavoury details, and yet she had called them in. She must have wanted to get the knowledge off her chest, out of her system.

"Drugs, Superintendent."

Ross MacAllister spoke without thinking, "So it *was* drugs!"

Hamilton looked at him, fiercely, and then turned his attention back to Mrs. Cummins.

"How do you know all this, Mrs. Cummins?"

"Her daughter. Her youngest daughter, Pauline. She writes to me."

"Is that the daughter in Australia?"

She nodded. "She went out there to get away from her mother. She's a nice girl. She found out, by accident. I don't know the details, but I think she found some cannabis resin in the Albany Crescent house, and saw some of the types who came."

"Types?"

"Stars. Singers. Pop groups . . . stayed

for the night on their way to the clubs to perform. Got the stuff from . . . from Hannah."

"And was she using the Albany Crescent house as a store for the drugs?"

"I don't know. I don't think so. When your chaps got pretty hot on the drugs types in Birmingham, I think she got frightened."

"Frightened?"

"Yes. Frightened of being caught. This . . . this sordid business wasn't known outside the family, Superintendent. I wouldn't have known, if Pauline hadn't told me. It all went on abroad, you know. All secret and well out of the way, until she started with drugs here."

"Did she take drugs herself?" The Pathologist hadn't mentioned drugs after the post mortem.

"No, never, thank God."

"When did she stop her drug supplies. Any idea?"

"I don't know . . . but . . . well, I wondered if that was the reason for her murder. You know, she stopped supplying people who went crazy . . . I wondered if they had done this against her for revenge."

"I see your point." Hamilton turned to Gwyn Thomas who had listened intently to the brief, but important story. "Think it's feasible, Gwyn?"

"If they killed her, sir," said Gwyn, "they'd be cutting off their own supply, surely?"

"But she had already stopped. So there was no supply—and yet think of these people, going mad with their cravings, coming to her and being turned away. Offering high prices for the stuff and being turned down . . . think of their mental state, Gwyn."

"Revenge?"

"Possibly. It's a good angle." He turned back to Mrs. Cummins, "This is invaluable information, Mrs. Cummins. Very important. Now, you mentioned her family being involved. What family do you mean?"

"Her sons, George and Eric."

"What about her husbands?"

"They divorced her—I think they found out what she was doing—except for the last one. He died. They didn't want anything to do with her."

"And the sons?"

"They were in business with her," and her head dropped. "They were such nice little boys."

"But surely they were too young to be involved in the brothels?"

"The early ones, yes. But not the later ones—the ones she was running recently. But their job was to circulate the drugs . . . they went all over the country, taking supplies."

"God!" cried Hamilton. "Gwyn, the photos."

Gwyn Thomas took the file from between himself and Ross MacAllister, and passed it to Hamilton.

"Mrs. Cummins," he said, "I have pictures of two men here—two men who were killed in road accidents on the same day as Mrs. Dowd. I'd like you to look at them and tell me if you know them."

He passed the photographs to her, watching her face.

She looked at them briefly and nodded.

"George and Eric."

"Her sons? The drug pushers?"

She nodded her head again, weary and fed up now. "They have different names because they had different fathers. George Wallace and Eric Hewitt. They used to be such nice boys. Such nice young men."

"She didn't have many friends?" commented Superintendent Hamilton as Mrs. Cummins absently passed the pictures back to him.

"No. She had none around here. No one bothered with her because she wanted to keep herself to herself. No one knew who she was—for obvious reasons. She didn't want to be recognized in Birmingham."

"Yet the press knew?"

"I told them, a long time ago. By accident . . . my husband was killed in a works accident . . . and somehow I let it slip that I was related to Annette Wallace who lived in Albany Crescent . . . well it all came out who she was. But I knew she wanted no one to know, so I made the press promise not to publish it. They said they would record it for when she died...."

"Ah! I see ... Good. Now we're getting somewhere," sighed Hamilton. "Mrs. Cummins. We haven't had the body officially identified yet—no one knows Mrs. Dowd sufficiently well. Could you? Would you come to the mortuary and identify her?"

"Yes," was all she said.

"And the two sons—they're in Leeds and York."

"I'd go along there, Superintendent. I'd like to see them again ... such nice boys ... you'd have to take me, though. I haven't got a car or anything."

"I would do that, with pleasure. Now, you've been most helpful, Mrs. Cummins. Most helpful. I'll send a car round for you, to formally view the body, then we can make arrangements for a trip out to York and Leeds, probably tomorrow. Is that all right?"

"Yes, of course. It's my duty."

"Before we go, Mrs. Cummins, there is one last question."

"Yes?"

"How well do you know her secretary—a Miss Joan Edwards?"

"I've never heard of her," said Mrs. Cummins.

14

"THE way I see it," said Superintendent Hamilton back at his office, "is that the Edwards woman knows all about the drugs and the brothels; she's probably the secretary of those businesses. She knows that we're on to her because we've connected the Leeds and York killings with the Birmingham one. So she invented a tale about her mistress returning tomorrow from Nice, and made us believe her by saying she didn't know that dead woman. I think she arranged the murders . . . got those long haired drug addicts to kill her victims."

"How?"

"By withholding supplies. If Eric and George were drug pushers, working with their mother under the guidance of the Edwards woman—she would know their routine in York and Leeds. It wouldn't be a difficult job for the killers to follow the men, or watch their movements. They steal a car, do the job, and come back here in their own vehicle."

"Why would she do it though?" put in Ross MacAllister. "Surely, if she killed the boss, and the two main shareholders, she stands to lose a lot of money?"

"Not if she assumes control herself and uses her own runners or pushers, as they are known in the trade. Besides, there's always the question of the will, isn't there?"

"It's a possibility," acknowledged Ross. "Have we found the name of her solicitors?"

"Yes. One of my men discovered it this afternoon—thanks to the newspaper. Firm of Davidson and McGee—Mr. McGee was her personal solicitor and knew her by both names. Unfortunately, he's away until Monday—and he's taken his safe keys. We haven't access to the will until he comes back."

"Is he out of the country?"

"Yes. Gone off to Scandinavia, touring with a caravan, otherwise I'd have brought him along to his office. He is expected to return late on Sunday night. Anyway, the will is in hand—and the Australian police have contacted the daughter in Australia. She's fit and well; she's not coming to the funeral. They've put a guard on her until we give the all clear."

"Have your men traced that youth, Rodney Hill, and his two companions?" asked Ross. "After all, they did the killings in York and Leeds."

"No. But we have circulated a picture of Hill and a description of his colleagues. Our uniform branch is taking pictures to every chemist in the city. We think one of them will try to get supplies of drugs from the chemists."

"Especially your late-night chemists," suggested Ross. "They'll emerge, like rats, under cover of darkness. Have you rounded up all your other pushers?"

"The Drug Squad is having a purge on every known addict, supplier and pusher in the city tonight. They've also given the house at Albany Crescent a thorough going over to see if drugs were there. They found nothing."

"So we must find Joan Edwards and we must find Rodney Hill and his mates. Any word from Leeds or York?" asked Gwyn Thomas.

"Nothing definite, I'm afraid. They traced both cars to Birmingham, you knew that."

"I did. Surely that's good circumstantial evidence that the Hill gang are involved?"

"It would be put forward as circumstantial evidence, but it might not carry much weight with some of our juries! Mind you, we've got to catch them first."

"But they are in Birmingham, aren't they?" asked Ross.

"My staff feel confident that they are," said Hamilton. "We've had road checks and so on. I think they'll have gone to ground here."

"Can't we have a purge of some sort?" suggested Gwyn Thomas. "A concentrated attack on suspect areas?"

"How?" put in Hamilton. "Every spare

man in the force is either on road checks or on the murder hunt, taking statements and attending to the routine stuff. So we can only wait and see—I think the drug angle is perhaps the best. Sooner or later they'll have to emerge to get supplies. Then we'll get them."

"Isn't it worth dragging one or two men off their routine jobs to concentrate on the night duty chemists?" suggested Ross.

"I suppose so—what about you, though? You've seen Hill. You've also seen the girl and the sharp faced individual, Slim. Fancy a trip round the chemists tonight?"

Hamilton laughed at the suggestion, but Ross said, "Yes, I do. I'd willingly go round them . . . but what about you, Gwyn? Ought we to get back to York?"

"I don't see why—we know the murderers are here, in this city, and they are wanted for a crime in our city. No, we're all right here. I'll willingly stay—mind you, I could do with a sleep. . . ."

"Me too!" yawned Ross.

"All right," said Hamilton. "I can fix each of you with a bed in one of our section houses. Get your heads down for an hour or two and you can do the all-night chemists tonight. How's that? And I'll put a couple of cars on too!"

"Suits me," said Ross, and Gwyn Thomas echoed his agreement by saying, "If I can take a killer back to York with me, it'll be worth it."

"He might be our killer too!" grinned Hamilton. "But I'll settle for Joan Edwards."

As they spoke, Joan Edwards was in London. Her escape from the police car had been too simple for words—a plea for the lavatory and the driver had so gallantly agreed to her request.

A taxi out of town; one or two changes of bus and then a train into London. This had earned her an uninterrupted journey and now she was hurrying through the streets of Crystal Palace to a small hotel which she knew quite well.

She carried no luggage other than a

handbag with some cash with which she had purchased sufficient toiletries to see her through tonight. Tomorrow, she had an appointment outside Claridges at three o'clock, and no police officer on this earth was going to prevent the appointment taking place!

A London transport bus took her almost to the door of the Sunlight Private Hotel, and she walked briskly towards it, occasionally glancing over her shoulder. But no one was around—no policeman had followed her. Why should he?

But they might if she'd let them drive her right home—they were like that. Always suspicious—they'd have made sure she was back in residence at Quarton and then kept a close watch. Followed her everywhere.

But now she'd dodged them, and she would keep her rendezvous tomorrow as arranged—and they wouldn't recognize her tomorrow.

She entered the small hotel, and rang the bell on the reception desk. A rather elderly man came from behind the curtain and asked her what accommodation she required.

"Just tonight, please. A single room."

"Sign the register please."

As he checked his rooms, she signed "Juliet Morrow, Coventry" and smiled at him.

"First floor, madam, number seven bedroom. It's got a washbasin."

"Thank you."

And she went upstairs happily. She wouldn't go out tonight, for she had a good book to read—a paperback.

Joan Edwards was happy. No one would find her here.

Somewhere in Birmingham, in a cellar, there waited three frightened youngsters, and one of them was lying on an old mattress, pale and stiff, limbs twitching spasmodically, and his eyes stared blankly at the ceiling, low and dirty.

"Rod, go and get a shot for me. Please . . . God! You must . . ."

"I can't! Every bloody cop in

Birmingham's looking for us . . . every bloody one. . . ."

"But I'm going crackers . . . I must . . . oh God!" and a throaty sigh erupted from his body. The limbs twitched and jerked; his long pale and pointed face was moulded with sunken cheeks and skin drawn taut across the bones, almost yellow in the dim light.

"When it's dark, Slim. When it's dark . . ."

"You go, Kathy. You go. They don't know you."

"That bloody MacAllister knows me . . . he knows us. He's put the spoke in. I said they'd cotton on. . . ."

"Get me some now, Kathy . . . please . . ."

She went across to Rodney Hill and spoke softly, "You'll have to get the poor bastard a shot or two, Rod. He'll go mad. I've seen him like this before . . . he's left his stuff at home sometimes; he goes wild."

"Where the hell can I get snow at this time of day? The coppers will have got their beads on all our places . . . they know us, Kathy. They know we're hooked and they'll know we need the stuff."

"The chemists: Break into a chemist's."

"Not me. Slim's got himself into this jam, so he'll have to get himself out."

"No, I can't, Rod. Can't walk . . . look at me . . . look at me!" His voice rose to a pitch, "Bloody well look at me . . . a wreck! Get me a fix of snow, will you? One will do . . . go and do a doctor's surgery . . . or a dentist. . . ."

"Please," said Kathy, "please," as she moved to Slim's side.

"But they know me . . . they've got my mug in their records. They don't know you, or Slim."

"I can't break into a surgery, Rod! And neither can Slim—look at him . . . just look at the poor bastard! He couldn't walk out of this dump!"

Rodney Hill didn't look. He had no need to. His friend, Slim, was twitching on a filthy mattress, eyes gaunt and staring . . . A wreck of a man at twenty-two years of age. Hooked since the age of fifteen. An addict to cocaine.

"Give me till dark. I'll go out at dusk. I know a doctor's place—new surgery in a quiet street, away from houses. I'll break in there."

"How long, for God's sake?"

"Couple of hours."

They looked down at Slim who didn't reply, but Kathy said, "He'll never last."

"He'll have to. It's my skin I'm risking."

In York, the basic routines surrounding the fatality were almost over and the accident report had been completed, although the more serious work was still to come. The Coroner had delayed the opening of the inquest until Mrs. Cummins could identify the body; even then he could open it for identification purposes only, which would allow the funeral to be completed, while further enquiries were made. The Leeds Coroner did the same.

In both cases, the outcome of the case

depended upon the results of the enquiries in Birmingham, and the capture of the killer or killers.

In support of the police, the Leeds and York press, both daily and evening, had given the twin fatalities a lot of useful publicity, and in York, it resulted in a landlady of a small boarding house near the Theatre Royal recognizing the deceased.

She rang York police station, and a detective was sent round to interview her.

"Yes, I wondered where he'd gone," she said, "I thought he had done a bunk—gone without paying, you understand. We get a lot of those types, but I had a look in his room and his case is still there."

"What name did he use?"

"Wallace. Mr. G. Wallace. It's in the register. He signed in."

"When did you last see him?"

"Half an hour before the accident. Twelve o'clock yesterday. He came in and said he was going to have a wash and a shave—very clean chap, he was. I don't do lunches, you see, and he said he was meeting a man in a café in York."

"Did he say which café?"

"No. But he was going to have lunch there, wherever it is. Anyway, he didn't come back. Then I read that bit in the papers and guessed it was my lodger."

"What was his business here? Any idea?"

"He didn't say and I didn't ask."

"Has he been here before."

"He said he'd come here about two years ago, but I couldn't remember him. Nice chap. Pleasant."

"When did he arrive then?"

"Wednesday evening. Had supper and bed on Wednesday; breakfast on Thursday. He went out after breakfast—about half-past nine. Came back at twelve for his wash and I never saw him again."

"Did he have a car?"

"Oh, yes. A smart sports car—a red one with a black roof."

"Where did he park it?"

"Dunno. I told him to use one of the

'Trust the Motorist' car parks in the city."

"You won't know his car again?"

"No idea. Just a red sports car."

"Thank you. Now, I'd like to take his stuff to the office, if I may. And I'd like a look through his room."

"Help yourself. He's dead, so he can't complain, and I don't want the stuff."

"Thanks—like to show me the room?"

The same applied in Leeds. The proprietor of a small public house on the road from Tadcaster was reading the evening paper before the influx of regular customers and he connected the death of the mystery man with the disappearance of a guest from his hotel. The dates and times tallied, and so did a description of the dead person.

Accordingly, he rang Leeds City police and told them that the man had booked in as a Mr. Eric Hewitt of Birmingham; the police said a member of the CID would call shortly for a statement, and to collect any belongings that he might have left, including the vehicle he'd driven upon his arrival. It was parked behind the pub—a nice Vauxhall estate car.

Once each set of luggage had been catalogued, checked and searched, a list of the contents was made. Birmingham City police were then asked to pass the information to Superintendent Hamilton. A wallet in the Leeds hotel contained two hundred pounds in notes.

The chain of evidence was growing.

But Superintendent Hamilton was no nearer to catching his killer.

Joan Edwards was safely installed in her London hotel, reading in blissful solitude.

Slim, the drug addict was in mental agony in a dingy cellar, but his friend was preparing to undertake a journey into the city to steal some cocaine.

It was almost dark.

15

ROSS MACALLISTER awoke with a start and found Gwyn Thomas standing over him with a mug of coffee in his hand.

Ross sat up quickly, wide awake now and asked, "What time is it, Gwyn?"

"Half-past eight, Friday night."

"Half-past eight? I've slept for hours...." He accepted the coffee with a brief word of thanks. "Hell! Time I was getting up."

"Don't worry. I've just struggled out of bed myself."

Gwyn Thomas settled on the side of Ross's bed as his friend drank the welcome drink.

"What's happened, Gwyn? Any developments?"

"Nothing. They've got a wonderful organization down here, Ross. I'm delighted at the way the city's police force has got this city sealed off. They've got a motor unit on every main road leading from Birmingham; they've got motor cycle check points, all radio equipped, on the smaller roads, and foot patrols at all other likely escape routes. Bloody efficient, you know—mind you, they've got the numbers to do it."

"That's where a large force scores over a small one, or over a rural one. Have they found Slim, the hatchet faced individual yet?"

"No. Not a whisper."

"Think he's got away before they had time to put the seals up?"

"Possibly, but knowing human nature, they'll have hidden up somewhere. Besides, if they're addicts, they'll have to be near supplies, won't they?"

Ross agreed with his friend, then asked, "What about the drug pushers in the city. Are they being given a turning over by the police?"

Gwyn Thomas grinned happily. "They don't know what's hit them! There's nearly a dozen of them in the nick now, under arrest for being found in possession of dangerous drugs. The police had given all their flats and homes a real going over and have confiscated their immediate supplies. But none of them admit knowing the whereabouts of Rodney Hill."

"Is he the main pusher?"

"No, just a supplier to lesser mortals. He gets his supplies from someone else . . . we don't know who that person is."

"It might have been Mrs. Dowd," said Ross.

"In that case he wouldn't have killed her, would he?"

"He might—if he could get his hands on her supplies—in other words, if he could take over her incoming drugs he'd make himself a useful sum of money."

"A possibility, but after the drugs squad have had a go at the pathetic creatures they've got downstairs, they seem to think there's another pusher somewhere. A big man."

"Do they, by jove!"

"There's even a suggestion he wanted Mrs. Dowd out of the way."

"What about Joan Edwards?"

"I don't think she enters into this side of the picture, Ross. Her name was given to the addicts downstairs and it didn't mean a thing."

"She might be the big boss, mightn't she?"

"Hamilton thinks she is."

Ross didn't answer. He sipped at the hot coffee, and said, "When I was with those addicts, Gwyn, there were only three of them. The girl, the man Hill and Slim. In the York car I saw Slim and Hill. In the Leeds car, there was a woman as passenger, so who is the fourth person? Who is the driver of the Leeds car?"

"We don't know, and the point hasn't escaped us. Hamilton has asked Leeds to have another chat with the woman who witnessed their accident, but it seems hopeless. I don't think she can make a positive identification."

"That doesn't surprise me. A fleeting

glimpse seldom identifies a person . . . if we could find Hill, it might be a help."

"If," sighed Gwyn Thomas rising from the bed. "And that is a big word. However, you and I have work to do."

Gwyn stood up. "We've got to drive round the city for an hour or two, peering into late-night chemists, in the hope you'll spot your friend, Slim!"

"He's no bloody friend of mine!" snapped Ross, climbing out of the bed. "But I'll gladly look for him. Have we a list of the shops?"

"Yes. The normal ones are closed now. Several stay open till ten o'clock, and one or two stay open all night."

"Think our friends will risk being seen in a well lit shop? I'd have thought they would break into a closed shop."

"We've circulated notices to this effect to all chemists, Ross."

"Good. Are we going in your car?"

"No. Hamilton's organized a radio equipped police car for us. Information Room know about our patrol, and they'll be keeping a listening watch for us. On top of this, the routine motor patrols of the city will be instructed to listen to our route, so we have to give our location every fifteen minutes. They'll be moving close to us in case we find anyone."

"Wonderful. Right, give me time for a quick wash and I'll be ready. I could do with a shave. My whiskers are a bit bristly!"

"Hamilton rustled up an electric razor —it's in my room. You can borrow that."

"We are organized, aren't we?"

Twenty minutes later they were on the road in a warm and cosy Ford Anglia. It was a pale blue colour with a radio aerial waving from its roof; Gwyn Thomas was driving and Ross sat beside him.

"Now, I don't know Birmingham at all well, Ross," confessed Gwyn Thomas. "But we've been given a large scale street map with all the late-night chemists shown as red dots. Can you look after that? Pinned to it there's a list of the shops."

"Got it. OK. Allow me to guide you through the streets. It's a bit like looking for a needle in a haystack, isn't it. Hell—there are dozens of these shops and the chances of us picking the same one at the same time as our addicts are pretty remote."

"What else can we do? Every policeman in the city is doing the self same routine, and this type of hunt has worked before. If those youngsters are in the city wanting drugs, they'll go mad to get them. That means sooner or later they'll have to emerge from their hiding place. It might take days, but when they do come out, it means they must be on some policeman's beat, so why not ours?"

"I can see that. Anyway, come along, Gwyn. Let's get moving."

They drove away from the brightly lit police station, into the city of Birmingham at night. Busy, bustling and active. People thronging the streets, shop gazing, walking or coming from late night work. Cars, buses, taxis. The place was alive.

Footsteps sounded on the stairs leading

down to the cellar where the fleeing trio waited. A double knock on the door and Hill said, "It's the Boss."

He opened the door and a stoutly built man in a clerical grey suit stood before them. He walked straight into the room.

"Got a fix for Slim?" asked Hill.

"No."

"Can you get one?"

"No. He's old enough to look after himself. Now, what's gone wrong?"

Rodney Hill looked at Kathy, who in turn looked at Slim, lying silently on the mattress, twitching and staring fixedly at the ceiling.

"The cops. Found our place and flushed us out. We got the bloke who saw us in York—name of MacAllister—but he got away. They know us now."

"They know you, but not me," said the Boss. "I went to your house. Saw them—they're still outside now, so I came here. So they know about York and Leeds."

"They do. They know the lot. . . ."

"God! And I thought they'd never guess...."

"They wouldn't," cried Kathy, "if it hadn't been for that man MacAllister. He saw Slim outside Albany Crescent and recognized him. He witnessed the York accident."

"Outside Albany Crescent...?"

Kathy fell into silence as the Boss turned and stared down at the helpless Slim.

"And what the hell was he doing there? The bloody idiot!"

He walked across and suddenly brought down his hand across the addict's face; Slim's head rolled from side to side and the staring eyes remained open and unflinching; there was no other reaction.

"I ought to kill him... I ought to dispose of that lunatic now...."

"No!" shrieked Kathy. "No, please. No, you mustn't. He's ill."

The Boss stood silent, heavy set and menacing, looking down at the pathetic form of Slim. "He's no good. He's no good as a person. No good at all. A cabbage. A liability. He ought to be destroyed!"

"No, you can't. You can't!" Kathy stood between the Boss and Slim, defiant and beautiful. "You can't do it."

"Why is he like this?"

"He wants a fix! He's overdue. Rodney's going out to get some."

"Going out?"

Kathy spoke, "He'll go mad shortly, will Slim. Then he's liable to do anything. He's as strong as ten men when he's mad. He'll run out or something. Rodney must go. Now."

"Have you brought any?" Rodney Hill asked the man they knew only as the Boss.

"Not likely. The cops are everywhere —they've got a dozen or more addicts or pushers in the cells, all screaming out for fixes and they're watching all our known customers. I can't get him anything."

"Then it's up to you, Rodney. If you don't, Slim will go himself—and in this state he's not responsible for what he does."

"No," said the Boss, "Rodney can't go. He's known to the cops. Known as a pusher. They've got his mug in their records. You'll have to go, Kathy."

"But I can't. I can't break into a shop!"

"Then you'll have to learn. Those are my orders. Your picture is not in any police records . . . you must go. Then if Slim does start anything Rodney will be able to control him. All right?"

She nodded.

Rodney Hill spoke, "There's a doctor's surgery on the corner of Vyner Street, Kathy. Square, modern place, with a car park. Little windows at the rear—easy job to get in."

"You've done it then?" asked the Boss.

"Long time ago, when I was starting on the racket. He keeps all sorts—plenty of cocaine. Slim's on cocaine."

Kathy nodded and said, "I'll go. How long does it take to walk there?"

"Fifteen minutes. Not much more. Know the way?"

She nodded.

"Off you go, then. Good luck, Kathy,"

wished Rodney Hill. "Keep your eyes open for the cops."

Kathy left the dingy cellar, climbed the steep steps to the floor above and left the old house. Above them lived six families of Pakistanis, who worked in factories in the locality, a dingy, filthy area.

She walked rapidly away from the place, turned left twice and was in a wide thoroughfare, full of lights and people. A club; a public house or two. Shops.

She stopped at a zebra crossing, waiting for a gap in the traffic; two buses, and a white Jaguar.

The buses were past. The Jaguar was level.

She saw the driver. The Boss!

Driving slowly over the crossing in the wake of the buses, with a gorgeous auburn haired woman beside him. She'd never seen the Boss like this . . . he invariably arrived unannounced, anonymous and blunt. She turned to gaze at the departing car.

She saw the registration number six, followed by letter G. Then it was obscured by the next car. And then she crossed the road and turned along the footpath at the other side.

She could still see the Jaguar, moving slowly through the late evening traffic; it indicated that it was turning left, to the Club Fiesta. It turned through a narrow opening which led behind the club, to the car park.

She made a mental note of this; it would give her the opportunity to identify the man who had now assumed control of the supply of drugs in the Midlands. The man who had arranged the deaths of Wallace and Hewitt, and undoubtedly that of Mrs. Hannah Dowd, the woman who stood in his way.

Then the Jaguar was gone, lost in the darkness behind the club premises, and Kathy hurried on her mission.

She found the surgery without any bother. It was new and compact, built on the site of a war damaged house, and she walked around it, briefly examining the place.

She'd been with Slim when he'd broken

into places, and knew a little bit about how to do it—but this place was isolated. Away from houses. A few warehouses stood to the rear.

She went round to the back, dark and quiet, and found a toilet window. Small and made of thick glass, it was on the ground floor and promised an easy entry for her. It was hinged, and would open sufficiently for her to climb through. She was slim.

But first she had to smash the window; she could see the brass catch inside.

She looked around; nothing.

Then an idea. Her shoe. She took it off, then listened. Silence. A car passing somewhere near. Next she slipped off her cardigan and placed it against the glass; it would deaden the sounds of her hammering.

She brought the heel of her shoe hard against the thick glass, it had no effect. Again.

This time the glass gave; it cracked across its width, and she gave the stubborn window a third crashing blow and the glass shattered and fell to her feet.

Using the shoe, she lifted the catch—she'd learned about the value of fingerprints and then she climbed in.

It was very dark . . . and she hadn't a torch. Might be one inside though. Or a candle—but she had matches.

She struck one; found the latch on the toilet door and emerged into the passage.

Then she saw the door marked "Office". It was standing open and just inside she found a keyboard.

Then the match died and she dropped it to the floor. She struck another and found a key marked "Store".

She sighed with relief and took it from the board.

But Kathy was unaware of the burglar alarm which had been built into the surgery. The place was regularly broken into by persons in search of dangerous drugs, and the police had suggested an alarm which warned them, but not the criminal. And the doctor had complied—

he had fixed an alarm which told the police of any intruder.

So, as Kathy had climbed through the toilet window, the alarm told the Information Room of Birmingham City police exactly where she was.

A message was relayed to a patrol car of the Drug Squad, and it was heard by Gwyn Thomas and Ross MacAllister.

"This might be our friends, Ross. Let's go. A surgery in Vyner Street, they said."

"Got it on the map," announced Ross. "Less than a minute from here, Gwyn. Take the next turning on the right."

And Gwyn Thomas accelerated to the scene.

"This is probably just the break we need," he said softly. "Just the break."

16

"HERE it is. Slow down, Gwyn."

Ross had seen the sign showing Vyner Street and asked Gwyn to stop. "Look, Gwyn. They'll be in there, won't they? Still inside...."

"Possibly."

"Let me go round on foot, while you hide the car. I think we should follow them—see where they're hiding up."

"That's assuming it is our suspects."

"Who else? They've got all the other addicts terrified . . . it's a chance we must take. If it's not one of our lot, we'll lose nothing except a little time."

"OK. You go on foot. There'll be other cars here any moment—I'll hold them off for the time being."

As Ross left him, Gwyn Thomas reversed gently away and parked the car in a back street. He radioed Information Room and asked them to prevent cars going direct to the surgery; by all means let them provide a backing power, he suggested.

As he spoke, a Wolseley drew up near him and he flashed his lights at the driver.

As Gwyn left the car to speak with the crew of the Wolseley, Ross MacAllister found the surgery and was circling in the shadows. It was low and squat, with large square windows. All of them were secure. The method of entry must be at the rear, or through the roof. The rear of the surgery backed on to the high wall of a large warehouse.

So in order to leave the surgery grounds, the intruder would have to come out by the front.

Ross waited, hidden in the dark shadows of a derelict building; his watch showed quarter past nine. Quite suddenly, he thought of Maureen, alone at home. He hadn't telephoned her since his morning call.

The children would be in bed and she would be watching television or sewing, or perhaps just waiting for his call. She'd be sitting by the telephone, anxious—he must ring her at the first opportunity.

Then a movement at the far side of the building; a sudden movement; a flash of blonde hair.

Someone peeking out to see if all was quiet. Ross pressed back into the shadows, turning his head into the cover of darkness as far as he dare allow, and then she was emerging.

A girl. Blonde and pretty, about twenty. He knew her—the girl, Kathy, he'd seen last night. A friend of Slim and Rodney Hill. . . .

Once she was away from the building, she began to increase her pace and Ross noted that she carried nothing. Had she found drugs? Was that what she'd been seeking?

Ross began to follow. She returned to the street in which Gwyn Thomas and the others waited; Ross hoped she'd turn away from them and she did. She turned left, hurrying into the gloom, and Ross went after her. Then he realized he could give no indication to Gwyn that he had found the girl. . . .

He could run back, but he might lose her. . . .

But Gwyn Thomas had foreseen this; he waited on foot in a shop doorway and saw Ross and the girl. At this he gave instructions to the Birmingham car to move away and take up observations at the distant end of this particular street.

The Birmingham crew knew the exit, but could not identify the girl from their own knowledge of the drugs fanatics in the area. As Ross followed her out of sight, the Squad car turned away to accomplish its part of the shadowing operation.

Gwyn Thomas radioed control and gave them the details to date; he asked that Superintendent Hamilton be notified.

He then moved his car in the wake of Ross MacAllister, keeping well out of sight and coasting where possible along this deserted back street. It wouldn't be easy to maintain contact.

Hamilton received the message with glee; his big round face burst into a happy grin and he said, "Good. I'll get a few squad cars to keep watch on them. Bloody good show. Those Yorkshire chaps are doing a good job for us."

"It's for them as well," said his next-in-command, Detective Chief Inspector Crispin. "Think she'll lead us to their base?"

"If all goes well, she will. I only wish someone would lead us to Joan Edwards' base!"

"I've had a word with the Airport Police Headquarters, and they're keeping a watch on all the airports," Crispin told him. "No information from Buckinghamshire—they're watching the house at Quarton and there's nothing doing there."

"What about the search around Warwick—where she got away?"

"Drawn a blank. Nothing at all."

"I wonder if she's in London, Inspector?"

"London, sir?"

"Yes. Tomorrow is Saturday, and tomorrow she is supposed to be meeting her mistress. Remember—three o'clock outside Claridges."

"Yes, I do remember."

"I was just wondering if she was going to meet anyone else at that place and time. Just a thought, Inspector."

"Such as who?"

Hamilton shrugged his massive shoulders. "No idea. But she told us about the routine of meeting Annette Wallace, and she has never yet admitted that Annette Wallace is dead. So she might still go to London to meet Annette Wallace—or the person who is returning on the Nice flight."

"Worth a check, sir. I agree. Shall I get in touch with the Metro?"

"No. I think we should do that little job because we know what Joan Edwards looks like. We can identify her—they can't. So I think I'll have a run down to

London first thing in the morning and do a bit of snooping around."

"Good. Let's do that. I wonder how that Ross MacAllister fellow is progressing? He'd make a good detective, wouldn't he?"

"He's a fool if he joins the police force, sir! You get no home life!"

"He doesn't seem to get much as it is, judging by what Inspector Thomas was telling me. Still, it's nice to have members of the public like him."

Then the telephone rang.

Hamilton picked it up. "Superintendent Hamilton."

"Warwickshire County, sir. Detective Inspector Wisdom. A fisherman in our area has just reported finding a blood-stained hammer in a river—dredged it up in his net. Fresh, by the look of it. I wondered if it could be connected with your killing."

"More than likely—near enough too. Has he touched it?"

"No. Sensible type. It's just as he

found it—in his net. He's brought it along to the office."

"Fine. We'll need a statement from him, and we'll need the hammer up here. I'll have to see if one of our cars can come along for it."

"Don't bother. Our Superintendent has to come to Birmingham on an enquiry tonight—security thing. He'll drop it in your office."

"Wonderful! We'll have the blood checked and see if it has any prints on it."

"It has, almost certainly."

"Where was it found, Mr. Wisdom?"

"Ten miles outside Birmingham—near Kingsbury, in the River Tame. I'm speaking from Kingsbury now—it's on the A423 road, a few miles south of Tamworth."

"I know it. You stationed there?"

"No, I'm at Nuneaton."

"OK. You'll do the necessary with the statement? What time will the hammer arrive here?"

"Within an hour, sir."

"Excellent. We'll get cracking immediately. Stroke of luck is that. Many thanks."

Crispin had a look of delight on his face. "Wonderful news. Let's hope it bears fruit. Sounds very much like the weapon we're seeking—could a woman wield a hammer like that, sir?"

"It has been known, Inspector. Not very often, but it has been known. If the blood group of the deceased corresponds with that on the hammer, we're half-way home. If those prints correspond as well with Miss Edwards—well, there's no doubt at all."

"It can't have been in the river long, can it?"

"Depends on the state of the river. If it is smooth running, it would take a long time to wash away dried blood. And the killing was only yesterday—the hammer might have been there only a matter of hours. We'll just have to examine it carefully and learn as much as we can. Now, I wonder how MacAllister's coping?"

The girl was hurrying along a side street, and never once did she glance behind; suddenly she was in a brightly lit area, with lights and shops all around. Ross followed; he saw the police Wolseley with a plain clothes crew. It was parked in a pub car park not far away and as he passed, he noticed they were speaking into a microphone.

Opposite him was the Club Fiesta, and the girl glanced at it. For a moment, Ross thought she was heading for it, but instead she paused at a pedestrian crossing, then swiftly crossed the road.

He did likewise; as he checked the traffic, he saw Gwyn Thomas in the line of waiting cars and acknowledged him with a swift nod of his head.

Gwyn responded accordingly, and Ross was across the road now, dodging people who were coming and going along the busy road. He had no difficulty following her—her blonde hair was a signal for him, and she turned down a side street. Now she was heading for the poor drab area which was hidden behind the glittering façade of the main street.

Five minutes later, Ross was feeling nervous; he was in a dark, badly lit street. Coloured people eyed him suspiciously; they eyed the girl, too, and Ross thought he might have to go to her rescue; but none of the men approached him or the girl.

Then she was home. She crossed the dark road and made for a tall Victorian house with iron railings. Steep steps led to a brown front door. There was filth on the windows, paint hanging from the door and woodwork. She hurried up the steps, her feet clattering noisily.

And then all hell was let loose.

Two men hurtled from the house. She was knocked over as they screamed out of the place; two men locked in a bloody fight, one of them heaving like a wild animal.

He was screaming, clawing, foaming at

the mouth, crying, "Get them . . . get them . . . they're after me. . . ."

"It's that hatchet faced swine!" cried Ross as the men tumbled down the steps. The girl was on her feet scrambling down now, but the man was mad, mad, mad.

He had his companion on the floor, beating, crying; there was a brick in his hand, and it was coming down again and again on the other man's head.

"No, Slim . . . she's here . . . she's got a fix for you . . . no . . . no! God . . . he's mad."

And down came the brick again; Ross heard it crunch into the unprotected skull of the man on the ground as the crazed madman cried, "Get me some . . . get me some . . ."

The victim ceased his struggle and Ross ran forward crying, "Stop it, stop!"

But Slim had turned on the girl.

"Give me the snow . . . give me it. . . ." He was snarling at her, foaming at the mouth, his hands clawing at the air like talons as he advanced towards her, with the brick poised high, ready to strike.

"I got it, Slim," she whimpered. "In my handbag . . . a fix for you . . . God, you're crazy! . . . No!"

She screamed.

He raised the brick and brought it down, shrieking obscenities as he battered the girl about her head.

Ross leapt on to his back, reaching at his throat. But Slim had the strength of a lunatic and shook Ross as if he were a piece of rag. The brick came down again on the girl, felling her, and then there were car lights, blue flashing lanterns, men running. Blood.

Six of them overpowered the crazy youth called Slim; Ross attended the girl.

The left side of her face had been battered by the vile brick wielded by her maniac friend; she lay unconscious at the side of the street.

Gwyn Thomas was beside Ross.

"She's the girl in that flat, Gwyn. Kathy is her name. She's the girl who broke into the doctor's surgery to get drugs for that swine over there. He's crazy . . . mad. God! Look what that foul stuff can do to a man."

A car raced away and from it came sounds of hoarse screaming and loud thumping. A madman fighting for freedom, for the release which only cocaine would give him.

Two of the Drug Squad men were kneeling beside the battered Rodney Hill, and one of them shook his head.

"I think he's nearly had it, sir. We've radioed for an ambulance—this is Rodney Hill. Makes a living smuggling drugs to the addicts . . . he deserves everything he gets."

The girl was groaning and Ross had an arm beneath her, supporting her battered head.

"Kathy," he spoke softly to her and her eyes flickered.

"She'll be all right," said Gwyn Thomas. "Her mate over there's a bit dodgy, though. Where did they come from Ross?"

"The house with the brown flaking paint, Gwyn."

"I'm going in to have a look round." And he moved towards the bleak premises calling two uniformed constables to accompany him inside.

Whilst he was away, the ambulance arrived and the injured couple was placed inside. Two members of the Drug Squad accompanied them after a verbal battle with the ambulance crew. But the Squad men won and joined the couple on the journey.

Ross went towards the house as the car containing the maniac addict was driven off at high speed to a police doctor, who would give the man an injection.

He met Gwyn Thomas coming out.

"It's a houseful of Pakistanis, Ross. Except for the cellar—a fly ridden, damp hole of a place with little more than a foul bed and a couple of chairs. Seems those three arrived sometime last night and according to one of the inmates here, the slim faced lad used to live in the cellar. He got kicked out for non-payment of rent—the house is owned by one of the Pakistanis who live here. The place was never let again—but they just moved in last night."

"Do we know his name?"

"Slim. But we can find out more now. They've taken him to a doctor for an injection and then we'll see what he has to say."

"Three of them, Gwyn! Those two men are definitely the men who ran down George Wallace in York."

"The girl was in the Leeds car. I wonder who the other man is and where he's got to."

"I haven't the faintest idea. Come along. Let's get back to the office and tell Superintendent Hamilton. He'll be delighted!"

"The girl will have to be interviewed, won't she, Gwyn."

"About the Leeds job—that's a job for Leeds City, I suppose."

"Can't we do that for them?"

"I suppose we could—we can see who

was with her and who ordered the killings. And why!"

"She might tell us quite a lot, Ross. Quite often a woman will cough the lot when she's cornered. I hope your little Kathy does."

"She looks quite nice, Gwyn."

"Aw, come off it, Ross. A woman like that? Mixing with killers and drug pushers. Hardly your sort of girl!"

They were walking towards the car, leaving the local men to search the cellar and question people in the locality about the activities of the girl and her companions.

"She's not my sort of girl at all, Gwyn. But I think she looks nice—I was wondering how she got involved in this sort of a carry-on. She doesn't look the type."

"It takes all sorts to make a world," grunted Gwyn Thomas as they reached their car. "Come along. Stop mooning about her and let's get back to base."

Detective Superintendent Hamilton was overjoyed.

"Marvellous!" he beamed. "Wonderful! Just when I thought I'd come to a dead end, everything is coming out right!"

"Something else happened, sir?"

"Yes. While you were busy arresting your drug addicts, a fisherman found a hammer. It's almost certainly the one used to kill Mrs. Dowd."

"Where is it?"

"In our lab. We've had a Forensic chap dragged in from the pub to get to work on it. He should have some news shortly."

"Good. Now, I'd like to interview that girl," put in Gwyn Thomas, "and the two men, if they both survive."

"All in good time, Gwyn Thomas," smiled Hamilton, "all in good time. The thin one is under sedation in a cell at the moment, fast asleep; the other one, Rodney Hill, is unconscious in hospital and so is the girl."

"So we're nearly finished with the hunting now. All that remains is the questioning," said Ross.

"Not as simple as that. You might get your killers, but mine is still missing. We still don't know who killed Hannah Dowd, do we?"

As if in answer to his query, the door opened and Doctor Ian Smith, the Forensic expert, strode in.

"Good news, Mr. Hamilton," he said in his soft well spoken voice. "The blood on the hammer is the same group as that of Mrs. Dowd. There's no doubt about that. Both group 'A'."

"Good. And the fingerprints? Are they any good?"

"Two very clear ones—the thumb and middle finger of the right hand. Very clear. I'm sure your men can photograph them now. They should be good enough to establish an identity."

"I'll ring our fingerprint experts. Thank you, doctor. I'm sorry to have spoiled your night out."

"Nonsense, Superintendent. Pleased to help. Now, I'll get back to my wife in that pub. Good-bye."

"You'll let us have a formal statement in due course?"

"Naturally," and he was gone.

"Fingerprint chaps next," and Hamilton rang for them.

By ten o'clock the fingerprint men had photographed, classified and checked the prints against the records kept in Birmingham.

"Well?" asked Hamilton.

"They belong to a man, sir. A labourer, because the skin is rough and broken in places."

"A man?" cried Hamilton.

He wondered where Joan Edwards came into the story.

17

"THE girl's come round, Ross, and the hospital says she's fit to be interviewed. I've got the job—there's a police-woman with her all the time. Hamilton says you can come."

"Fine. What about the men—Hill and his addict friend?"

"Hamilton's interviewing Hill; the addict is still under sedation."

"Good. Let's go then."

Inspector Gwyn Thomas and Ross MacAllister reached the hospital, and the sister on duty showed them to a ward where Kathy had been placed alone. A pretty police-woman sat by the bed.

As MacAllister entered, the girl turned her head into the pillow, shouting, "No, you bloody man! It's all your fault!"

"Nice welcome for you, Ross," chuckled Gwyn Thomas. "I thought you had a way with women?"

"I think you invented that, Gwyn!" And they settled down beside the bed. Kathy, her face bandaged down the left side, was morose and unco-operative; the police-woman said nothing.

Gwyn Thomas spoke:

"Hello, Kathy, how's the head?"

She didn't reply, so Gwyn persisted, "Kathy, I am Detective Inspector Thomas from York and the position is this: Three murders have been committed and we know that you are involved in at least one of them. You were seen in a car in Leeds which ran down and killed a man. We have a witness. The penalty for murder is life imprisonment, Kathy. Now, I want to know who was driving that car. I want the name of your driver."

She didn't answer.

"We know who was driving the York car—it was Rodney Hill and we know who the passenger was. We know who killed Mrs. Dowd, and now we can prove that you killed the man in Leeds. Scientists have examined the car."

"I didn't drive it! I didn't! God knows

I didn't. I wanted nothing to do with the accident . . . nothing!"

"Who made you, Kathy?"

She was weeping softly into her pillow, a sorry sight of a girl, and Ross spoke now, "You've nothing to be afraid of, Kathy. We shan't disclose who informed us, and at least we can ask for leniency in court. We can tell the judge how co-operative you were. . . ."

"But I didn't want to go . . . I didn't . . ."

"Who was it, Kathy?"

"I don't know!" she screamed and beat the pillow with her fists, "I don't know his name!"

Gwyn looked at Ross. "Describe him then?"

She turned over and rested on an elbow, facing them. Her eyes were red rimmed and sore, her face pale and unhealthy.

"I don't know his name," she said softly. "He's the Boss. Everyone calls him the Boss."

"The Boss of what?"

"The drugs. Getting the drugs. He gets them—I don't know where from—and he sells them to the pushers."

"What's he look like?"

"Getting on a bit—nearly forty, I'd say. Nasty piece of work—round face."

"Much hair?"

"Thin, but not bald. Brown hair."

"Fat, thin? Untidy? Beard?"

She shook her head, "Just ordinary. Bit fat, I think—always smart."

"Where does he hang about? Clubs?"

She nodded, "I saw him tonight—he went into the Fiesta Club with a lovely woman. She had a mass of auburn hair—it was gorgeous," and for a brief moment, Kathy smiled.

"Was he walking?"

"No. He has a white Jag. It's lovely."

"I suppose you don't know the number."

"No. Except it's got a six—that's all. Just a figure six in the number and a letter 'G' at the end."

"Wonderful. Now, what's he do? How's he organize his drugs?"

"I don't know. He does it through Rodney. They meet somewhere and Rodney sells around town. I don't know . . . I don't know. . . ."

Ross spoke, "You seem a nice girl, Kathy. Not the sort to get mixed up in this sort of thing."

She started weeping again, "I did it for Slim. . . ."

"Slim?"

"The boy who's been taken away. The addict."

"What's his proper name?"

"Robin Spender."

"Your boy friend?"

She nodded. "I joined up with them because I thought I could help him . . . he was so badly hooked . . . it's terrible. But I started experimenting with the soft drugs—you know—purple hearts and that sort of thing, and then on to cannabis. I managed to stop in time. Slim didn't."

"He's in a bad way, Kathy," said Gwyn Thomas quietly. "Now, back to this man called the Boss. He was with you in Leeds?"

"Yes. He told me we were going to collect some stuff in Leeds, while Hill and Slim did the same in York. So I said I'd go."

"Did he use his Jaguar?"

"No. He had another car...."

"A fawn one? A Vauxhall?"

"It might have been. I don't know."

"Sorry. Go on, Kathy."

"Well, we got to Leeds and waited outside a gent's barber's shop and then this man came out. The Boss watched him and said, 'That's the man I want.' Then when the man was walking along the main street in Leeds . . . well . . . the car got on to the footpath and knocked him down . . . oh, it was horrible!"

"And he didn't stop?"

She shook her head. "No, he didn't. He didn't stop! The swine . . . I hate him for it . . . I hate him for what he's done to Slim . . . and others like him . . . I hate him. . . !"

"Is he the only supplier in Birmingham?" asked Ross.

"I don't know," she whispered.

"Did you know Mrs. Dowd? The lady who died yesterday?"

"I'd heard of her."

"Did she supply Rodney Hill?"

"I think she did. I don't know though. I just don't know."

"Well, I think that's all for now, Kathy. We might want to see you again," said Gwyn Thomas. "Now, I'll have to have your full name please," and he took out his notebook.

"Kathleen Riley and I live at 67 Colstan Road, Edgbaston."

"Age?"

"I'm twenty."

"Occupation?"

"Out of work; I work in a factory as a rule, but they've closed down the part where I worked."

"All right, Kathy. I'll be back to see you. Now, you get some rest and don't worry about anything else."

"Thank you, sir," and there was the

faintest trace of Irish in her accent. "It was nice to tell somebody about it."

Outside, Gwyn Thomas asked, "What do you think of her now, Ross?"

"I still think she's not the sort to get involved in a set of circumstances like the present one, Gwyn. Not the sort at all."

"You think she was telling the truth then?"

"Of course I do."

"Good. So do I. Now, we must find Hamilton and see what he's got out of those lads. Then we'd better organize a raid on the Club Fiesta."

"Hamilton might know the chap with the white Jaguar, Gwyn."

"May well do. Come along. Let's get back to the office."

Superintendent Hamilton hadn't had much luck. Rodney Hill was an experienced crook who would never admit anything which could not be proved. He refused to believe that anyone had positively identified him in York and he denied having stolen the Ford Escort which had caused the fatal injuries.

Hamilton had then left him, under the eagle eye of a watchful constable, and was enjoying a cup of tea in the office when Gwyn Thomas and Ross returned.

"You chaps must have smelt this tea," he said. "Help yourselves to a cup out of the cupboard; there's plenty in the pot."

As they drank, they told him their story and he was cheerfully happy now.

"Good!" he said at length. "The Boss? I wonder who he is . . . large white Jaguar. Can't bring it to mind. Hang on. I'm going to have another go at Hill—I'll mention the Boss."

He went back to the cells and confronted Hill once more.

Hill was looking confident. "Now, Super. Come back to have another go, have you?"

"We've got some more information since I saw you, Hill," Hamilton told him. "We've found out all about a man called The Boss, and his system of supplying drugs to you. Nice little deal you had, eh?"

"The Boss! You found him?"

"At the Club Fiesta," put in Hamilton, hoping that this meant something to Rodney Hill. "We identified him by his white Jaguar and the auburn haired beauty he carries around with him."

"Oh God! This is the end!"

"And we've got Kathy, remember. She's quite talkative, too. Didn't want to get tangled up with you lot in the first place, but did it for Slim, she said."

Hill fell into a long silence, thinking deeply. Hamilton waited—an experienced policeman knowing full well that Hill was deciding whether or not to tell his story. And Hamilton could wait. He could wait a week if necessary. Or a year.

"I drove the York car," he said. "On the Boss's instructions. We had to winkle out George Wallace and run him down at half-past twelve."

"How did you know he would be on the bridge?"

"We left a letter at his digs. Told him

to meet us just after twelve-thirty. We knew he'd cross the bridge about then."

"A call to die, eh. And you ran him down."

"I was ordered to . . . by the Boss."

"Why was Slim with you?"

"To make sure I did it. He's hooked—he'll do anything for a fix."

"You stole the car in Birmingham—we've found it with false number plates."

"I'm sorry, Inspector," said Hill suddenly and quite out of character, "I'm sorry."

"You've been honest enough to admit your part in the York fatality—we know about the Leeds one. Now, what about Mrs. Dowd, here in Edgbaston?"

He paled noticeably. "Now don't try to pin that one on me, mister Inspector. I know nothing about that one. Nothing at all."

"Did you know she was George Wallace's mother?"

"Good God, no!"

"And the mother of the man killed at Leeds by the Boss."

"Hell!"

"So if the Boss organized the York accident and the Leeds one, it looks as though he organized the Edgbaston one as well, doesn't it?"

Hill nodded. "But I don't know . . . God. I've admitted one. Isn't that enough?"

"No! I want the man who killed Mrs. Hannah Dowd. We've found the weapon —a hammer."

Hill didn't flinch. "Good. I hope you catch the bastard who did it."

"We will. We've got enough evidence now."

In his office, Hamilton turned to Gwyn Thomas and said, "You've got your accident solved, Gwyn. Well done. A crime neatly solved; so have Leeds. I'll get Crispin to ring them and tell them, although we haven't got the Boss yet. Let's go, shall we?"

"Where to?"

"The Club Fiesta, of course. We can get there and back by the time the fingerprint men have found our suspect—that's if he's got a previous record."

"Off we go then."

On the way, Gwyn Thomas asked Hamilton how he intended to deal with the Boss—a man whose name he did not know.

"I didn't ask Hill because it would have shown how *little* we know, so I'll ask at the door. Ask the doorman . . . and go on from there."

In the club car park, they found the Jaguar—KOO 6 Z, and Hamilton went towards the doorman of the Club Fiesta; people were still entering the flashy club for a late session of dancing, gaming and drinking. Ross waited outside the Club doors as Hamilton and Gwyn went inside.

"Whose is the white Jaguar?" asked Hamilton.

"Who wants to know?"

"I do. Police!"

"Oh, white Jaguar! Er, Mr. Justin St. John, sir. You know—he has the gents' shop in town, and a carpet factory. Very nice man."

"I'd like a few words with him—I've got some bad news for him."

"If you ask at the reception desk, sir—they'll put you in touch with the floor manager. He'll find Mr. St. John for you."

Hamilton strode across the carpeted foyer of the club and he could hear music in the background, soft and gentle. The place was warm and clean; there was an aura of wealth about it.

"I'd like to speak to Mr. St. John please. It is urgent business."

"Mr. St. John?"

"Justin St. John—he's inside. Can you ask him to meet me here, in the foyer?"

"Just a moment, sir. What name shall I give?"

"A friend. Tell him it's a business colleague with bad news."

She was back in a minute and said, "The floor manager is seeking him now, sir."

"Thank you."

Five minutes later, a thick set man in

a smart suit emerged from the club room, clutching a large cigar between his lips.

Hamilton saw the receptionist point towards him, and St. John came his way, his brow creased in curiosity.

"Hey," he said, "who are you? And what's all this about bad news?"

"The name is Hamilton. Detective Superintendent Hamilton, and I have to warn you that you are not obliged to say anything unless you wish to do so . . . you are under arrest for conspiring to murder Eric Hewitt in Leeds at twelve-thirty yesterday afternoon."

"Catch me!" said St. John and he stood in the foyer with a tiny pistol in his hands. "Just try to catch me, copper!"

And he backed towards the door and his waiting car.

18

OUTSIDE the doors, Ross MacAllister saw the sudden dangerous movement of their prey. Inside, Superintendent Hamilton stood absolutely still, trying to decide on the best method of attack upon this dangerous man; Gwyn Thomas moved away from the Superintendent, looking for an opening.

The people in the foyer froze with fear; a woman screeched and St. John was shouting, "Come and get me . . . just you try . . ."

He was a couple of yards inside the swing doors, edging sideways towards them, one eye on the menacing police, the other on the exit.

Ross waited. St. John was a mere yard inside, shouting abuse and defiance at the police officers. His eyes were on them.

Then Ross crashed open the doors; it

startled St. John who swung round with the revolver in his fist, but Ross dived at his feet in a flying tackle.

St. John fell; the gun exploded and a bullet ricocheted from the marble walls into the ceiling; Hamilton pounced like a lion and so did Gwyn Thomas who swiftly disarmed him.

"Now," Hamilton spat at St. John, "we can go."

The report about the fingerprints on the hammer had come through. It proved that the bloodstained hammer had been in the hands of a man called Roger Dunstable, aged twenty-four, who had seven convictions for robbery with violence and assault with intent to rob. His prints were on Birmingham police records.

Detective Inspector Crispin knew the man; he passed a message to the night duty Town Inspector and asked that Dunstable be brought in for questioning.

He would probably be in the Durham Ox, half drunk and wanting to fight someone. The Town Inspector said,

"Right. I'll fix that. And I'll take four men with me!"

He was as good as his word.

An hour later he rang back.

"I've got Dunstable, Mr. Crispin. He wasn't at the Durham—we found him at home. Like a frightened kitten, he was. Offered no resistance at all."

"Where is he now?"

"In our cells. Shall we bring him over?"

"Do you mind?"

"Not at all."

Dunstable admitted killing Mrs. Dowd; he had no choice because the fingerprints gave away his secret and St. John readily passed the blame to him.

"Midnight," said Hamilton, "and all our killings solved—but we haven't found Joan Edwards."

"Do we need to, sir?" asked Gwyn Thomas.

"I think we do. I think she's mixed up

in the affair, somehow, Gwyn. I'm sure of it."

"Have any of the other culprits mentioned her name?"

"No. No one. I find that puzzling. If we hadn't found this chap Justin St. John, I'd have sworn Joan Edwards was the killer . . . or the organizer of the killings, at the very least."

"Shall I cancel the messages that are out for her arrest?" suggested Gwyn Thomas.

Hamilton pursed his thick lips and twirled the tip of his flamboyant moustache with his fingers.

"Nope," he said eventually. "No. She told a pack of lies about the identification of Hannah Dowd, alias Annette Wallace; she has signed a statement giving false information, and that amounts to perjury. I warned her about that when I took the statement. We can take action on that alone, if nothing else turns up. Then she disappeared from our police car. Why? If she has nothing to be afraid of, why run away?"

Ross MacAllister spoke, "Perhaps she was frightened to begin with—frightened you would arrest her for the murder. And remember, women do strange things."

"Nonsense, Ross! That woman's involved somehow and I mean to find out. All that nonsense about booking trips abroad!"

"Did you check the writing on that postcard with the entries in Mrs. Dowd's books—those you found in Albany Crescent?"

"One of our handwriting wizards had a look at the two sets of writing," Hamilton added quietly. "They were undoubtedly written by the same person."

"Which suggests that Annette Wallace is abroad, like Joan Edwards said."

"Nonsense!" bellowed Hamilton. "She could have written that card anywhere and sent it abroad for posting."

Ross nodded. "Of course, I should have realized that!"

Gwyn Thomas came in. "What do we do now, sir? It's getting late."

"I have no intention of chasing all over

the countryside tonight to turn up Joan Edwards," said Hamilton. "I'm going to bed—I can do with some sleep. My subordinates can finish off the clerical work; I've got staff at the hospital watching the injured parties. The rest of them can spend a night in the cells, and I'll charge the lot tomorrow with murder. What about you chaps?"

"But Joan Edwards . . ." said Ross.

"She was going to meet her mistress outside Claridges at three o'clock tomorrow. We know her mistress is dead, but just suppose that Miss Edwards is telling the truth! Suppose that she did not honestly recognize her mistress, she'll be outside Claridges, won't she?"

Gwyn Thomas nodded. "It's a possibility."

"I've seen the woman—I know her by sight—so tomorrow I shall take a trip into London to see her. I will be outside Claridges at three o'clock to see what happens. I might also meet the noon plane from Nice to see who gets off it

—to see who has flown over on Annette Wallace's reservation."

"Good idea. At least that should clear up some puzzles." And Gwyn Thomas looked at his watch. "Ten past eleven, Ross. We can be back in York by two-thirty or so, if we leave now."

"God! I haven't rung Maureen!"

"Then you'd better do it now, hadn't you?" chuckled Hamilton.

"Are we going home, Gwyn?"

Gwyn Thomas nodded. "Yep. I think we'd better. We'll have to arrange an escort from York to fetch our prisoners back and fix another from Leeds. We need Slim and Hill; Leeds want St. John and the girl."

"Pity we couldn't take them back now, isn't it?"

"We haven't the transport, Ross. No. We'll do it in the official manner. Now, you ring Maureen, then we'll be on our way."

In spite of the late hour, Maureen sounded relieved to hear his voice; Ross muttered profuse apologies about his prolonged absence, and she accepted them, albeit grudgingly.

"It will be late," he said. "We shall leave Birmingham in a few minutes—be home about three."

"I won't wait up," she had said this so many times before. "Are you sure you'll come this time?"

"Promise," and he made kissing noises into the phone, then rang off.

"Right. That's it then," said Hamilton and he shook their hands. "A few good crimes cleared up. I've a lot to thank you chaps for."

"All in a day's work," said Gwyn Thomas. "And at least I've got some results to show my Chief."

"And I've enjoyed visiting your city," chipped in Ross. "Hope you'll pay us a visit, Superintendent Hamilton. Briar Cottage, Ryethorpe—drop in if you find yourself in Yorkshire's prettiest valley!"

"I'll do that, I promise. And thanks again."

"You'll tell me what happens about

Joan Edwards, won't you?" requested Gwyn Thomas.

"I'll do that with pleasure. Give you a ring, Gwyn."

And they left the office. Ten minutes later, they were heading north through the night. Gwyn Thomas was driving and Ross had promised to take his share at the wheel, but for the moment, he was fast asleep. Gwyn Thomas had no intention of rousing him—Ross's children would see to that in the morning!

Superintendent Hamilton was at London Airport to meet the twelve noon flight from Nice. His warrant card gained him admission to the administrative offices.

There he learned that Annette Wallace's seat reservation from Nice to London had not been cancelled, although someone else had taken the seat—this was not objected to, provided the person who booked it did not mind.

The incoming person had given the name of Miss Louise Armstrong of South Kensington.

Hamilton waited. He had primed the customs officials to tell him which was Louise Armstrong and now he waited in a glass doored office, watching the incoming passengers.

Then the signal.

A customs officer raised a hand, palm towards him, and Hamilton saw a young woman, tall and slender, with a head of jet black hair tied in a bun. She wore smart rimless glasses and a dark blue overcoat. She carried two suitcases of luggage.

With an airport police-woman in close attendance, Hamilton left the office to meet the woman.

He caught her as she emerged from Customs clearance; her luggage had not been inspected.

"Miss Armstrong?" Hamilton addressed her almost casually.

"Yes?" She turned to face him; a tall beautiful girl of about twenty-six.

"We are police officers," he told her. "My name is Hamilton."

Her face fell; she paled visibly, and her

beautifully manicured hands began to shake. "Would you mind stepping into the office?"

"Why? What's happened?"

"We'll explain inside. It will be easier."

She accompanied them into the office and he closed the door.

"It is Miss Louise Armstrong?" He spoke the name slowly.

"Yes."

"Do you know a woman called Annette Wallace?"

"Yes. I do. Why?"

"I understand you travelled on her seat reservation?"

"Yes. She came home on an earlier flight—I got her seat. There's nothing wrong in that."

"No. But she's dead, Miss Armstrong. She was murdered on Thursday."

"No! You can't mean that? Oh, God . . . why?"

She looked around the room; Hamilton pushed a chair towards her and she flopped into it.

"What is your connection with her?"

"I work for her—in Nice. At a club."

"A club?" queried Hamilton.

"Yes, a club!" snapped Louise Armstrong. "I'm a hostess!" He knew what she meant.

"When was she last there?"

"Last week. She came home last Saturday."

"Thank you. Now, I must search your luggage."

"My luggage? But the Customs have cleared it."

"Then you won't object!"

She shook her head. "What are you looking for?"

"Drugs," Hamilton was brief and blunt.

He found them. Neat little packets sewn into the linings of suits and dresses; sewn along the hems and shoulders; sewn into the sleeves.

The girl denied knowledge of their presence, but that didn't make any difference.

Hamilton arrested her, and vowed he would meet a few more planes in from

Nice. He left her in the custody of the airport police for the time being.

At ten to three he was sitting in his car with a good view of Claridges' main entrance, and he felt sure he would not be noticed by Joan Edwards.

At five minutes to three, there appeared before the hotel a dingy woman in tattered clothes. A stooping, dreary individual wearing thick black stockings and a huge floppy brimmed hat.

Hamilton watched her; if this was a disguise, it was hopeless because it served only to draw attention to the person wearing the awful clothes; he watched closely. He felt sure it was a disguise. . . . Joan Edwards?

There was no sign of the Joan Edwards he knew. Two minutes to three.

Unless . . .

Then he saw the face beneath the floppy hat . . . the woman looked up to peer across the street and he saw her features.

"It's her!"

He almost left the car to go immediately to her, but changed his mind.

"Let her wait . . . let's see who she is meeting. . . . And why in disguise?"

Then he realized—she must have guessed someone would be here to watch her. She must have anticipated police interest in her visit.

The shabby figure paced up and down, walking a trifle too easily for the type of person portrayed by the disguise. The minutes ticked by. . . .

No one came to meet Joan Edwards.

No one.

Had Hamilton been close, he would have seen tears in those eyes; they were tears of sadness. Tears of utter disappointment.

At five minutes past three he went across to talk to her.

She didn't run away this time.

19

AT six o'clock on the Saturday evening, Ross MacAllister's telephone rang. He jumped up to answer it, but Maureen said, "Oh, no! It's Saturday night—I want to have a little bit of time with you!"

"You answer it, then," he said, playfully smacking her bottom.

She hurried at its call, and seconds later was back, saying, "It's a Superintendent Hamilton—says he wants to tell you what happened in London today—no snags attached!"

"Oh, lovely. Right, this is the end of the story, Maureen. I must find out what Joan Edwards was up to."

Hamilton sounded quietly pleased with himself and said, "Nice to hear you again, Ross. I can't get Gwyn Thomas—perhaps you'll tell him the news. I met the Nice plane and caught a drug smuggler coming in on Annette Wallace's reservation. Seems this is a regular arrangement—woman from her overseas brothel coming in with the drugs. I'm having earlier flights checked with a view to tracing other women—they're all prostitutes, I'm sure. Taken abroad from this country, and then flown back to retirement, or with drugs. Quite a racket—it seems the journeys were booked in Annette Wallace's name by Joan Edwards—quite innocently, it seems."

"Innocently?"

"Yes. Joan Edwards is quite innocent. I've had words with her about the affair, and she's absolutely innocent. She booked the return trips, but invariably Annette Wallace flew home a week early, under the name of Hannah Dowd. She did this to keep her dirty secret from Joan Edwards."

"Then Joan Edwards knew nothing about the Birmingham address or the name of Hannah Dowd?"

"Nothing at all. I'm convinced she knew nothing about the sordid history of her mistress either, and I'm equally certain Annette Wallace did her utmost to keep the secrets from her. This carry-on about meeting outside Claridges—the plane gets in at noon, yet Joan Edwards had strict instructions never to go to the airport—Claridges was the meeting place and that meant Joan Edwards never knew that her mistress came home a week earlier."

"It seems a complicated way of keeping a secret."

"Wait, Ross. Remember that Wallace had business interests in Birmingham. So what she did was to fly in a week earlier than expected and spend that week in Birmingham. She took her drugs there, and her sons distributed them for her."

"I see. Then she came back to London in time to meet Joan Edwards outside Claridges—as if she'd come straight from the airport."

"That's it."

"But didn't Joan Edwards ever go abroad with her?"

"Once or twice on genuine holidays,

but never on business trips—her mistress always made the excuse that she liked to keep Joan at Rock House, Quarton, to keep things in order there. And Joan Edwards did just that—she was an efficient secretary and, in fact, Annette Wallace has one or two legitimate businesses in England. She was a wealthy woman in fact."

"Who benefits from the death then?"

"The daughter in Australia gets everything, even though that girl cast herself away from her mother. It seems her mother recognized the good character of the girl and has left her everything as a reward. But there is provision for Joan Edwards. She gets an income for life from the capital and she gets a lifetime's free use of Rock House. So she'll be all right."

"I find it amazing she knew nothing about her mistress's other life?"

"Very few people did. It was so complete—so cleverly done. Annette Wallace took extreme pains to make sure no one did know—I'm sure she was horrified at the depths to which she had sunk to make money, simply to keep up appearances."

"But why did Joan Edwards lie about the identity of Hannah Dowd?"

"The woman she saw was Hannah Dowd; in other words Annette Wallace without her make-up, without her fine clothes; she was away from her usual surrounds and she looked so different. But there was a likeness and I feel that Joan Edwards guessed, but was uncertain about the truth. I think she had some idea of the deception at that stage. I think she knew her mistress was involved in something shady and by denying that the dead woman was her mistress, it gave her time to sort things out in her own mind. That's why she ran away from our car—she didn't want the police checking on every move she made. She wanted to find out the truth for herself in her own way and in her own time."

"You'll go ahead with the perjury charge then?"

"No. She wasn't too sure about the identity—and as far as we are concerned, it did us good, didn't it? It made us delve a little deeper into the life of Annette Wallace. It made us prove beyond all doubt that it was one and the same woman."

"And Joan Edwards accepts this now?"

"She does."

"Good. Oh, the motive, Superintendent. It was drugs then?"

"Yes. Hannah Dowd, alias Annette Wallace held the supply monopoly in the Birmingham area and others wanted to cash in. But she was too well established and had such good contacts through her theatrical friends, that her competitors found her difficult to dislodge. On top of her position, she undercut her rivals' prices too."

"I thought she'd given up dealing in drugs, though? I thought she was killed by jealous addicts, or something."

"No, far from it. She was still going strong, undercutting Justin St. John and others. It cost her her life."

"But surely they warned her off? Surely

men like him weren't frightened of a little old lady?"

"No. They threatened her time and time again. . . ."

"Until they had to kill her, eh?"

"I think she wanted them to kill her, Ross. I think she was so utterly ashamed of her past. . . ."

"You'll never prove that, will you?"

"No. Never. But it's a nice thought, isn't it. Good-bye."

"Good-bye," and Ross MacAllister replaced the receiver. He went back to Maureen and settled on the settee beside her, placing an arm around her and pulled her to him.

"It's nice to have a cosy home," he said.

"It's nice to have a husband," responded Maureen MacAllister.

Other titles in the
Linford Mystery Library:

A GENTEEL LITTLE MURDER
by Philip Daniels

Gilbert had a long-cherished plan to murder his wife. When the polished Edward entered the scene Gilbert's attitude was suddenly changed.

DEATH AT THE WEDDING
by Madelaine Duke

Dr. Norah North's search for a killer takes her from a wedding to a private hospital. She deals with the nastiest kind of criminal—the blackmailer and rapist!

MURDER FIRST CLASS
by Ron Ellis

A new type of criminal announces his intention of personally restoring the death penalty in England. Will Detective Chief Inspector Glass find the Post Office robbers before the Executioner gets to them?

TREAD WARILY AT MIDNIGHT
by Margaret Carr

If Joanna Morse hadn't been so hasty she wouldn't have been involved in the accident, and wouldn't have offered hospitality to the injured woman, only to find she was an escaped inmate from the local nursing home.

TOO BEAUTIFUL TO DIE
by Martin Carroll

There was a grave in the churchyard to prove Elizabeth Weston was dead. Alive, she presented a problem. Dead, she could be forgotten. Then, in the eighth year of her death she came back. She was beautiful, but she had to die.

IN COLD PURSUIT
by Ursula Curtiss

In Mexico, Mary and her cousin Jenny each encounter strange men, but neither of them realises that one of these men is obsessed with revenge and murder. But which one?

LITTLE DROPS OF BLOOD
by Bill Knox

It might have been just another unfortunate road accident but a few little drops of blood pointed to murder—and plunged Chief Inspector Colin Thane and Inspector Phil Moss into another adventure.

GOSSIP TO THE GRAVE
by Jonathan Burke

Jenny Clark invented Simon Sherborne because her daily gossip column was getting dull. But when the society editor demanded a picture of the elusive playboy, Jenny knew she had to get rid of him. Then Simon appeared at a party—in the flesh! And Jenny finds herself involved in murder.

HARRIET FAREWELL
by Margaret Erskine

Wealthy Theodore Buckler had planned a magnificent Guy Fawkes Day celebration. He hadn't planned on murder.

A FOOT IN THE GRAVE
by Bruce Marshall
About to be imprisoned and tortured for the death of his wife in Buenos Aires, John Smith escapes, only to become involved in an aeroplane hi-jacking.

DEAD TROUBLE
by Martin Carroll
A little matter of trespassing brought Jennifer Denning more than she bargained for. She was totally unprepared and ill-equipped for the violence which was to lie in her path.

HOURS TO KILL
by Ursula Curtiss
Margaret went to New Mexico to look after her sick sister's rented house and felt a sharp edge of fear when the absent landlady arrived. Her fears deepened into panic after she found the bloodstains on the porch.

THE DEATH OF ABBE DIDIER
by Richard Grayson
Inspector Gautier of the Sûreté investigates three crimes which are strangely connected—the murder of a vicar, the theft of a diamond necklace and the murder of Pontana's valet.

NIGHTMARE TIME
by Hugh Pentecost
Have the missing major and his wife met with foul play somewhere in the Beaumont Hotel, or is their disappearance a carefully planned step in an act of treason?

BLOOD WILL OUT
by Margaret Carr
Why was the manor house so oddly familiar to Elinor Howard? Who would have guessed that a Sunday School outing could lead to murder?

THE DRACULA MURDERS
by Philip Daniels

The Horror Ball was interrupted by a spectral figure who warned the merrymakers they were tampering with the unknown. Then a girl was ritualistically murdered on the golf course.

THE LADIES OF LAMBTON GREEN
by Liza Shepherd

Why did murdered Robin Colquhoun's picture pose such a threat to the ladies of Lambton Green?

CARNABY AND THE GAOLBREAKERS
by Peter N. Walker

Detective Sergeant James Aloysius Carnaby-King is sent to prison as bait. When he joins in an escape he is thrown headfirst into a vicious murder hunt.

VICIOUS CIRCLE
by Alan Evans

Crawford finds himself on the run and hunted in a strange land, wanting only to find his son but prepared to pay any cost.

MUD IN HIS EYE
by Gerald Hammond
The harbourmaster's body is found mangled beneath Major Smyle's yacht. What is the sinister significance of the illicit oysters?

THE SCAVENGERS
by Bill Knox
Among the masses of struggling fish in the *Tecta*'s nets was a larger, darker, ominously motionless form . . . the body of a skin diver.

DEATH IN ARCADY
by Stella Phillips
Detective Inspector Matthew Furnival works unofficially with the local police when a brutal murder takes place in a caravan camp.

STORM CENTRE
by Douglas Clark
Detective Chief Superintendent Masters, temporarily lecturing in a police staff college, finds there's more to the job than a few weeks' relaxation in a rural setting. He soon gets involved in a local police problem.

THE MANUSCRIPT MURDERS
by Roy Harley Lewis
Antiquarian bookseller Matthew Coll, acquires a rare 16th century manuscript. But when the Dutch professor who had discovered the journal is murdered, Coll begins to doubt its authenticity.

SHARENDEL
by Margaret Carr
Ruth had loved Aunt Cass. She didn't want all that money. And she didn't want Aunt Cass to die. But at Sharendel things looked different. She began to wonder if she had a split personality.

MURDER TO BURN
by Laurie Mantell
Sergeants Steven Arrow and Lance Brendon, of the New Zealand police force, come upon a woman's body floating in the water. When the dead woman is finally identified the police begin to realise that they are investigating a fascinatingly complex fraud.

YOU CAN HELP ME
by Maisie Birmingham
Whilst running the Citizens' Advice Bureau, Kate Weatherley is attacked with no apparent motive. Then the body of one of her clients is found in her room.

DAGGERS DRAWN
by Margaret Carr
Stacey Manston was the kind of girl who could take most things in her stride, but three murders were something different – especially as she had the motive and opportunity to kill them all . . .

THE MONTMARTRE MURDERS
by Richard Grayson

Inspector Gautier of Sûreté investigates the disappearance of artist Théo, the heir to a fortune. Then a shady art dealer is murdered and the plot begins to focus on three paintings by a seemingly obscure artist.

GRIZZLY TRAIL
by Gwen Moffat

Miss Pink, alone in the Rockies, helps in a search for missing hikers, solves two cruel murders and has the most terrifying experience of her life when she meets a grizzly bear!

BLINDMAN'S BLUFF
by Margaret Carr

Kate Deverill had considered suicide. It was one way out—and preferable to being murdered. Better than waiting for the blow to strike, waiting and wondering . . .

BEGOTTEN MURDER
by Martin Carroll

When Susan Phillips joined her aunt on a voyage of 12,000 miles from her home in Melbourne, she little knew their arrival would germinate the seeds of murder planted long ago.

WHO'S THE TARGET?
by Margaret Carr

Three people whom Abby could identify as her parents' murderers wanted her dead, but she decided that maybe Jason could have been the target. Then Abby was attacked in the old ruins and she wondered if she could be wrong after all.

THE LOOSE SCREW
by Gerald Hammond

After a motor smash, Beau Pepys and his cousin Jacqueline, her fiancé and dotty mother, suspect that someone had pre-arranged the death of their friend. But who, and why, and above all, how?

CASE WITH THREE HUSBANDS
by Margaret Erskine

Was it a ghost of one of Rose Bonner's late husbands that gave her old Aunt Agatha such a terrible shock and then murdered her in her bed? The Bonner family felt that only Inspector Septimus Finch could catch the killer.

THE END OF THE RUNNING
by Alan Evans

Lang continued to push the men and children on and on. Behind them were the men who were hunting them down, waiting for the first signs of exhaustion before they pounced.

CARNABY AND THE HIJACKERS
by Peter N. Walker

When Commander Pigeon assigns Detective Sergeant Carnaby-King to prevent a raid on a bullion-carrying passenger train, he knows that there are traitors in high positions within the railway, banking and even police circles.

Other titles in the
Linford Western Library:

TOP HAND
by Wade Everett

The Broken T was big enough for a man on the run to hire out as a cowhand and be safe. But no ranch is big enough to let a man hide from himself.

GUN WOLVES OF LOBO BASIN
by Lee Floren

The Feud was a blood debt. When Smoke Talbot found the outlaws who gunned down his folks he aimed to nail their hide to the barn door.

SHOTGUN SHARKEY
by Marshall Grover

The westbound coach carrying the indomitable Larry and Stretch and their mixed bag of allies headed for a shooting showdown.